The Mermaid and her King

Scarlet Wolfe

Mary,
You're so sweet. I'm happy you found your king in this huge ocean called life!

Scarlet Wolfe

Copyright © 2013 Scarlet Wolfe Books
All rights reserved.
This is a work of fiction. Names, characters, places and incidents either are products of the author's imagination or are used fictitiously. Any resemblance to actual events or locales or persons, living or dead, is entirely coincidental. No part of this book may be reproduced in any form or by any electronic or mechanical means including information storage and retrieval systems, without permission in writing from the author. The only exception is by a reviewer, who may quote short excerpts in a review.
ISBN-13: 978-1491096703
ISBN-10: 1491096705

Contents

Dedication..1

Notes..2

Chance or Fate..3

Plan Put in Motion 23

Rejection and Drive 34

Friend or Enemy 43

The Rubdown 55

A Second Chance..63

King of the Castle 72

Nixie 83

Angel of Temptation 90

The Tide Turns 105

A Do Over..117

Confessions...134

Explorations 145

More than a Mere Taste.......................................161

One Riveting Day..174

A Shower of Reassurance 183

A Love Note and a Boat 194

A Secret Kept 214

Back on Board 227

Layers of the Soul...233

You Read My Mind 240

Happy Birthday 247

My Worst Nightmare 256

Self-Destruction	266
Christmas Blues	268
Last Ditch Effort	274
Finding Chase	284
Self-Loathing	290
Brooke is Heaven	299
Messages from the Past	306
Finding Skyla	319
New Year's Eve	326
End Notes	331
Acknowledgements	332

Dedication

To those who brave the murky bottom of their souls.

Notes

This novel is written from the points of view of Chase, Skyla and Eric.

Chance or Fate

Skyla

My feet sink into the sand, and I stop to watch, digging my toes in farther. It's the oceans way of telling me to respect it, or it will swallow me whole. Unfortunately, I was given that message loud and clear nine months ago.

As I frequently stroll this beach at night, the moon has become my companion. It's my anchor to the ocean, the light allowing me this time to think. It's the only friend I have on this Hawaiian island.

Eventually, I pull my feet from the sand and start walking again. My bed is beginning to call for me since I have a sizeable house cleaning job tomorrow.

A little farther, and I'll turn back. After a few minutes, I hear laughter, and my heart begins to race when five shapes appear before me.

"Damn, you're hot. What are you doing on the beach so late?" He looks to be in his early twenties and so do his four friends.

"Hi. I was taking a walk, but I'm leaving now."

They stand only a couple of feet away from me. The one who spoke has a big grin on his face and is definitely cute, but that doesn't change the negative vibe I'm getting.

"We can't see a girl as attractive as you and let you run off. I think you're going to have to stay here and keep us company."

The other four guys form a half moon around me, and I feel the suffocating lump forming in my throat. The moves my dad and brother taught me to protect myself are not enough to fight off five guys.

If I had to guess, I'd peg them as drunk frat boys on vacation, but they seem too comfortable here. I bite my bottom lip and crinkle the side of my sundress in my fist.

Sweet talk is my only chance. If I can get the grinning asshole alone, I might stand a chance at running.

"Get the hell away from her. She was headed back to my place," a deep voice says from behind me in the darkness.

I see the intimidated look on the group of men's faces, so I spin around swiftly. My hair blows right into my face. I try to get the strands out of my wet mouth as I focus on the male walking toward us.

He's extremely muscular and tall with dark skin and black hair. I can see from the moonlight that it's silky. His Hawaiian heritage is obvious. Is he trying to help me out or get me alone for himself?

"Chase, what's up, man?" asks the guy who originally spoke to me. The crack in his voice is evident, and I sense a little fear.

"What are you doing out here?" Chase asks them as he walks up and stands next to me.

"It looks to me like she's going the wrong direction to be heading to your place, and you don't own the beach, Kalani," one of the other men reply.

"I think I've made it clear I own this part. She was about to turn around, so all of you need to take a walk."

I see the look he gives these men, and my gut tells me I'm safer with Chase. The way I see it, one guy is better than five.

The first man that spoke scowls. "You need to lighten up, Chase. You've been a real dick since ... well, you know."

"I'm going to be a dick if I think you're about to treat a woman like shit."

The man lets out a snorted laugh. "You're one to talk, dude. We'll leave your precious beach and woman alone. Come on guys."

I watch them walk away, and then I look up into the mysterious man's dark eyes for several seconds. He studies me without a word.

"I'm Skyla. So, am I safe with you?"

"You must think so, or you would've left with them. Can I ask why you're out here?"

"I was going for a walk."

"You risked your life to take a stroll on the beach?" he asks aggressively.

"No one's ever bothered me before."

"That's a ridiculous reason to think it's safe," he snaps.

Those guys were right about one thing. He does need to lighten up. "OK, it wasn't the wisest move, but if I want to take a stroll on the beach at night, then I have to go alone. I don't have any friends or family on this island."

His eyes narrow as if he's even more upset with me.

"Now, you've told a stranger that you're alone on Oahu. Where do you live?" He acts protective like my brother, Lee. Geez. My eyes take in his fit body in the moonlight, and I see his fists are clenched.

"Thanks for your help, but I can take care of myself from here." I begin walking.

"I asked you where you live," he says sharply.

I turn back around, preparing to unleash some attitude. "I'm not supposed to tell that to strangers." I whip my long blonde hair back over my shoulder and stare at him with my hands on my hips.

He's intimidatingly handsome. The kind of attractiveness you only see occasionally. That person who everyone's compelled to take a second glance at.

"You were last seen with me by Troy and his asshole friends, so I'm driving or walking you home. Your pick. I don't want the police at my door if you disappear."

I guess he has a point. Walking means having to speak to him longer, but driving means I'm trapped in his car. For all I know, he could be planning to sell me off as a sex slave. "OK, fine. I'd prefer to walk."

He stands staring at me again, so I take the lead. There are only a few dozen properties on the street that butts up to this stretch of beach. The property value of these homes are in the low millions.

Living on the North Shore of Oahu, Hawaii is peaceful. Unlike Honolulu, the North Shore is made up of small towns and is less populated. We walk thru a path that goes between two of the homes until we're out onto the street.

"I live only a couple more blocks from here. I'm sure I can make it alone," I say as I stop to look at him.

"No." His hands are in the pockets of his cargo shorts as he stares at me with raven eyes. I want to see what emotion lies in them, but it's too dark.

"What's made you so angry?" I continue walking with him by my side.

"The fact that you don't care one bit about your safety." He's mad at me and doesn't even know me. I glance up at him.

"I do care, but I told you that I don't have anyone else here."

He runs a hand through his hair and lightly growls. This man's giving me a complex. I walk up to my door, feeling his gaze on me the entire time.

Since he thinks he owns that part of the beach, I figure he owns a big fat house sitting in front of it, so I'm not thrilled he's seeing my dumpy place.

"Thanks for walking me home and getting rid of the creeps."

He stares at me from the end of the driveway. I think he wants to say something, but the silence only lengthens.

I give a half wave. "OK, goodnight."

"Goodnight, Skyla, and don't tell anyone else you're alone on this island," he demands before he walks away.

Once inside, I lock the door behind me. I wish I could get a look at his muscles in the daylight. I'm relieved it was dark walking home, otherwise, he would've seen me gawking.

Before going to bed, I make sure all the windows are locked. I don't like that Chase knows where I live. He didn't make me feel that much safer.

Chase

I finally get an opportunity to speak to her. She's the woman I've watched walk along the beach at night for months.

A woman who doesn't know me and all my bullshit, and I can't even say one nice thing to her.

I swear I want to lay her over my lap and spank that ass of hers for putting her life in danger. It's upsetting that her situation is even worse than I thought.

I mean, she's completely alone. Why is there not a male in her life to keep her safe?

I can't begin to imagine how pretty she must appear in the daylight. With only the light from the moon, her light blue eyes still stand out against her blonde hair. I'd love a better look at the awesome set of tits she's carrying, too.

I don't think Troy and his friend's would've hurt her, but I can't say with certainty. I saw from her body language that she was scared shitless. I couldn't allow that to continue.

Anyway, I'm selfish. I can tell she's different from the other bimbos I see on my stretch of beach, so if I can't have her, those dickheads aren't going to, either.

I definitely don't deserve her. At least my good deed got me a nice image to jerk off to.

Damn she's sexy, and I pray she'll keep coming back to the beach, but I'd prefer she do it during the daylight.

Skyla

Six comes too soon, so I hit the snooze button twice. The homes I clean are small, but this week I agreed to fill in for another housekeeper who gets to clean the larger, more expensive homes.

I only have to clean one of them, but from what I hear, I'll be there half the day. The snug, light blue tank top and denim shorts I put on, along with my hair up in a messy bun, are just right for managing the heat I generate from cleaning.

I'm using my brother's car while he's away on deployment, but I prefer walking whenever possible. The weather is too wonderful here not to. Combine my walking with the cleaning, and I get a pretty good workout.

After eating breakfast, I stuff my iPod into my pocket, grab my caddy of cleaning supplies and head out the door.

I clean the two smaller homes that back up to the beach, and then I start walking to the granddaddy of jobs I agreed to do.

As difficult as this job will be, I'm glad to get it. If I do well, I might get some other big homes to clean. They pay more and are more enjoyable to work in. If I have to clean windows, why not clean the ones that give me an awesome view of the ocean?

I'm not thrilled that I have to walk to the same area I was at last night. Glancing between the houses toward the beach, I cringe when I think of the scary men that could've hurt me if not worse.

Then I find myself daydreaming about the handsome and mysterious man who rescued me. I suppose he did, anyway.

As I approach the home that looks more like a mansion, I stop and stare in awe. I feel underdressed to even clean this place.

It appears to be the most expensive one along this stretch of road, and I guess it to be over ten million dollars easily.

I was told where a key would be hid for me to get in. I'm supposed to leave it on the counter and lock the door behind me when I leave.

I'm surprised I'm getting access to a key for any amount of time at a place like this. Finding it in a fake rock, I open the front door and yell to see if anyone is home, but no one answers.

Intending to do a quick walk through to familiarize myself turns into a twenty minute home show experience. The architecture is impressive, but the home looks like a bachelor's pad and feels cold.

I walk to the back of the house that butts up to the ocean and look out the floor to ceiling windows. The view is magnificent.

There are wide, sliding glass doors off the kitchen that lead to a patio with a short staircase that goes directly to the beach. I decide after soaking in my surroundings that I better get to work.

After turning up my music and popping in my ear buds, I begin in the downstairs bathroom. I finish the sink and start cleaning the bathtub, shower combo.

This one is small compared to the garden Jacuzzi tubs in the upstairs bathrooms, which are off each of the five bedrooms. I'm guessing this one is for those who come in from the beach.

I'm startled as someone taps me on the shoulder, which causes me to spin around. The problem is, only my body and one foot make it all the way around.

My other foot doesn't, so I lose my balance. The next thing I know, I'm falling back into the bathtub. It all happens so fast.

Here I lie, staring at a strange, attractive man whose face appears as terrified as I imagine mine does. He has golden blonde hair and big blue eyes. I say big because they are wide as I stare at him from the bottom of the bathtub.

I feel something dripping down my arm, so I look and see blood. My forearm caught on a metal hand rail on my way down, ripping my skin wide open. There's at least a four inch long gash down my arm that's gushing blood. I yank out my ear buds.

"Shit, are you OK?" the blue eyed guy asks.

"I think so, except for my arm."

His abs rock. He has to be a surfer.

"I'm sorry I scared you. You didn't answer me, so that's why I tapped your shoulder."

He stretches his hand to help me out of the tub. About this time, I hear another male voice. Great, an audience.

"Eric, where are ya, cuz?"

"I'm in here," the guy with me yells.

At least I know blue eyes name now, and those are some pretty blue eyes. Guy number two appears in the doorway.

"Damn, what's happening here?" he says before a smirk appears.

Eric turns to him. "Go ask grumpy where he keeps medical supplies. Tell him the housekeeper has a cut on her arm."

"Sure, dude." Guy number two disappears.

Seriously? There's a third guy? Didn't I experience enough embarrassment last night?

Eric helps me up and grabs a washcloth out of the closest to press against my arm.

I sit down on the closed toilet seat and hold the cloth to stop the bleeding. "I'm sorry. I shouldn't have had my music up so loudly. I'm fine, so you can go."

"No, I'm sorry. I should've yelled or something instead of touching you. I feel terrible because I didn't need anything. I just wanted to say hi.

"I'm not trying to sound like a perv, but your ass was sticking up in the air while you were cleaning, and well, it's a nice ass. I had to see the whole package," he says, giving me a boyish grin.

"Don't hold back there. Your honesty is refreshing." I shake my head and smile.

"It's my best and worst quality depending on the topic at hand."

Dang, his smile is as charming as his eyes. He looks to be a little older than my young twenty year old self.

"I guess you heard that I'm Eric."

"Yes, I'm Skyla."

"Nice to meet you, Skyla. You sure don't look like the Hilda beast. I guess she's off this week."

"If you're referring to the lady that usually cleans here, then yes, she's off this week."

Guy number two comes back to the doorway.

"He said there's a first aid kit in that closest on the top shelf."

"Eric, what'd you do to the poor girl? I'm Andy, by the way," he says, smiling.

"This is Skyla. I scared her, so she fell back into the tub."

Andy's good-looking, too, with his wet brown hair and hazel eyes. Like Eric, he's only wearing swim trunks and has abs that rock.

"Why'd you go and do that? She's too cute to injure." He gives me a flirty grin.

"I told her I was checking out her ass and wanted to see the whole package. I was right. Her face is even prettier."

"Shut up, Eric. Excuse him. He has no filter. I mean none," Andy says, sounding irritated.

Eric goes to the closet to search for what I assume is the first aid kit.

Chase

She's my damn housekeeper, so I guess I should be the one helping her. I walk up the stairs to the house, wondering what the two morons are doing. I hear them laughing when I get inside. She probably tripped over her orthopedic shoes.

I approach the hall bathroom and can't fathom why in the hell Eric and Andy are both in there with Hilda. She's a sweetheart, but the poor old thing is not attractive.

"What are you two doing?" I ask before I peer into the room.

Shit, it's her! What is she doing in my house and my bathroom?

She recognizes me. It's evident from the shocked expression on her face. Skyla. Just as I imagined, even more beautiful during the daylight.

"What did you two do to her?" I'm pissed. If they're the ones who hurt her, then they're in deep shit.

"I scared her. I didn't mean to, but she had her ear buds in and didn't hear me come into the bathroom," Eric answers.

"Tell him why you were in the bathroom," Andy says.

Eric walks over to her with the first aid kit.

"Shut up, Andy."

"It's my fault. I had my music up too loud and didn't hear him walk in."

She glances up at me but quickly looks away. She's protecting him. Skyla's beautiful *and* sweet.

"Eric was staring at her ass while she cleaned the tub. He wanted to meet her to see if she was the total package. He said her face was even prettier. Yeah, his words."

"Andy, I told you to shut up. I'm sorry, Skyla. It does sound bad when he says it. I shouldn't have told you that," Eric says.

"It's fine. Actually, it's flattering. I don't get compliments like that, so thanks."

She deserves a flood of compliments daily.

Oh, hell no!

Eric can't have her, either. I want to tell her not to fall for his bullshit.

"See, she liked it. My honesty is a good thing," Eric says, looking at me. He needs to get that grin off his face.

"Both of you get out. I'll take care of her."

Eric doesn't look up at me as he fishes through the first aid kit. "I got it, dude. Go back outside."

"No, get out. She's working in my house. I need to make sure she's OK. I think you've done enough damage."

I can tell he doesn't like what I said, but I don't give a flying fuck. He hurt the adorable creature. He isn't getting another minute with her.

"Fine. I'm sorry again, Skyla. I'll come back and check on you later."

"You don't have to do that, but thanks for helping me, and it's nice to meet you both."

I couldn't be happier to get their asses out of my house. They're my closest friends, but that doesn't change the fact that they royally get on my nerves sometimes. Shit. Now I'm alone with her. Maybe this isn't such a good idea after all.

"I'm really sorry to cause you more trouble. I'm able to doctor my own arm, so you can go back outside. I promise I'll get right to work after I bandage it up."

"Where's my housekeeper?" I open the gauze bandage and dig out a packet of antibiotic ointment.

"I'm filling in for her."

I grab a new washcloth from the closet and wet it. Holding her arm up, I carefully wash off the blood around her cut. I'm distracted by her addictive scent that's a cocktail of flowers, candy and sex.

OK, maybe I'm imagining the sex, but whatever it is has me excited. She turns her head up toward me. I shouldn't look at her face, but I can't resist. Those sky blue eyes stare back at me. Damn, she looks scared.

"Don't worry about working today. I'll tell the agency you did, so you'll still get paid."

She shakes her head at me. "No, I can't do that. This was my fault, and I'm perfectly capable of working. I don't even need stitches."

"You're not working. Your cut might get infected, so it needs to heal a little first."

"I'm a tough girl. I can handle a little cut. Do you always order people around and get your way?"

Sweet and sassy. I have the strong urge again to spank her ass among the other things I'd like to do to her. "I do tend to order people around, and I usually get my way. So, you're not working."

"Oh, I'm working," she says boldly, glancing back up at me. She's getting pissed, and I don't want her mad at me.

"You wouldn't be hurt if my friend hadn't been acting like a huge pervert. Please don't work today."

She better cooperate. "Please" isn't normally in my vocabulary.

Skyla

He's actually looking at me, and he said please. I feel like I'm doing something wrong if I don't work, but I have a feeling this is an argument I'm not going to win.

"OK, fine. I don't feel good about it, but I see it would be futile to try to talk you out of this."

He's dressed in a t-shirt, shorts and flip flops. Well, I think they call them slippers here. I'm puzzled as to why he isn't in swim trunks like his friends.

I wish he'd take his shirt off, too. From the look of his other muscles, I'm sure his abs are as impressive as his friends if not more so.

Taking his time, he doctors my arm. I inhale deep breaths, savoring the clean smell coming from him, but it's almost impossible to keep my breathing under control. After he cleans my cut, he puts antibiotic ointment on it and bandages it up.

"Do you live here alone?"

He glances from my arm to my eyes. His are dark and mysterious. He's intimidating, but I find myself wanting to challenge him. Shit, he probably thinks I'm trying to see if he's single.

"Yes."

"You have an awesome view. I'm sure you're aware of that and never take it for granted. I know I wouldn't.

I could stare at that water every minute of the day and never grow tired of it."

His eyes go back to my cut. I want Eric and Andy to return. They're friendlier and would make things less awkward. "I do have a great view."

Stated matter of fact with no visible emotion. Should I expect different? I search his eyes for something other than sadness, but he's an enigma.

I might be imagining, but it feels as if he dragged out the process of doctoring my arm longer than need be. Finally, he let's go of it.

"Thank you. I guess I'll go now. Sorry again for all of the trouble."

He nervously looks to the ground and back up again. "OK. Can I get your last name, so I'll know it when I call the cleaning agency?"

"It's Moore." After gathering my supplies, I walk to the front door. He follows me but keeps a fair distance between us. I turn and smile.

"Thanks for fixing up my arm and for paying me. I still don't feel right about it." Silence again. "Um, maybe I'll see you around sometime."

"Bye, Skyla."

I wish he would give something away. A smile would be nice. I shut the door, thinking maybe he wanted to say more …. wishing he would've said more.

Plan Put in Motion

Chase

The door shuts, and I feel something good inside. For the first time in months, I feel something other than guilt and pain.

Worthy or not, I have to find a way to keep her around for as long as possible. After the time I think it would've taken her to clean, I grab my phone off the kitchen counter.

"Hi, this is Chase Kalani. Skyla Moore just finished cleaning here. She did a great job, so I wanted to let you know. Also, I'd appreciate it if you would send Ms. Moore whenever Hilda's unable to work."

That was easy enough. The next part will be a little more challenging. I dial another number.

"Hilda, this is Chase. I wanted to make sure nothing was seriously wrong since you couldn't make it today. No, the girl did great. Your husband had to have hip surgery?

"That's terrible. Could I have your address? I'd really like to stop by in the next couple of days. I want to give you something."

I hang up, knowing I've reached a whole new level of pathetic.

Eric

After I finish surfing, I go into Chase's to check on Skyla. "Cuz, where's Skyla?"

"She's gone."

"Damn, I was going to ask her out."

"Don't."

"Why not?"

"Because I said," he replies, sounding irritated.

He really pisses me off sometimes.

"Chase, I've put up with your dictatorship attitude almost all my life, but we know you're not going to go out with her, so if I see her again, then I'm asking.

"We've already had the talk about what you're doing to yourself, so you know how I feel about it, but you can't keep trying to hold everyone else back, too.

"You need to get out of this self-pity bubble you're living in. If you don't stop punishing yourself, then you might as well have died with Bud."

I see his icy glare.

"Yes, I said his name. You need to hear it. It's been nine months, so it's time for you to start living again. You've lost almost a year of your life."

I go back down the steps to surf. I probably shouldn't get my hopes up too much when it comes to Skyla. I already sense that Chase likes her. I guess that would be a good thing.

He has punished himself long enough for Bud's death. Actually, a lot of other people punished him enough. He didn't need to add to it, but I guess the guilt he feels is still haunting him.

I'm glad Chase has made some positive changes, but it serves no purpose if he's going to stay locked up in that house.

Chase

Two days pass, and I can't wait any longer. After signing the check, I take a deep breath and slip it into my pocket. Hilda agrees to see me early this morning before she leaves to visit her husband at the hospital.

Driving down the road, I think about Skyla's striking blue eyes and fantasize about the cleavage I managed to stare at the entire time I was bandaging her arm. I might've stood there longer than necessary.

She hardly looked up at me, so I got to watch the top of those tempting, soft looking mounds shift whenever she moved.

They are the perfect size and need to be in my mouth, but my eyes are going to be the only thing on them.

I pull into Hilda's driveway and knock on the door. I feel bad to see that she lives in a shithole. She was my parents' housekeeper for years, and I don't understand why she's working for an agency.

I should've hired her privately, let her do more for me, so she could've made more money. I'll never stop being reminded of what a dirtbag I used to be.

"Chase, it's so nice to see you. Come in please. You've never wanted to come to my home before. Did I do something wrong?" She gives me a worried expression.

"No, Hilda. It's the opposite, actually. I owe you an apology. I haven't thanked you enough for all you've done for my family and me over the years. I should've paid you more."

She shakes her head. "No, Chase, you've been great to work for and very generous, and your parents were always so kind to me. Would you like something to drink?"

"No, thank you. I'm not going to stay. I'm sure you probably need to get to the hospital to see your husband. Do you remember the times you've mentioned to me about wanting to retire?"

Uncertainty spreads across her face. Oh shit, I've scared her. I have that effect on women.

"Yes, I recall we've discussed that many times, but I'm not able to retire yet. Maybe in another year or two. I have to take time off to care for Kamuela because of his hip surgery, so that will set me back awhile."

Her eyes search mine, and I can tell she's wondering where I'm going with this. I pull the check out of my pocket and hand it to her. I never have conversations like this. It's going to be uncomfortable as hell.

Her eyes grow five times their size, and I pray the check doesn't give her a heart attack. I can't take feeling responsible for another person's death. Bud's is enough. There, I said his nickname in my head. That's a start.

"Chase, I don't understand. What is this?"

"It's for you and your husband. Now, you can retire. You deserve it."

She tries to give it back. I'd counted on that happening at least a few times, but I get my way nine times out of ten, so I push her hand back toward her. Dammit, I'm going to have to say the mushy shit, so she'll keep it.

"Hilda, I've never been one to do for others. I've never given any money away other than to my friends, so I need to do this. My parents would be pleased, as well. I don't want you to struggle."

"Chase, I—"

"You've worked hard your entire life, so please keep this. Then you won't have to work anymore. You'll be here every day to take care of your husband with no worries."

"Chase, I can't accept this. I would've thought a hundred dollars was too much, and you're trying to give me a hundred thousand." She stares at the check in one hand while holding her other hand to her chest.

"Look. I don't like to hear the word no. This is as much for me as it is for you. You have to take it. I won't accept you not keeping it. If you tear up my check, I'll go to the bank and have it deposited into your account. Let me do this for you and your husband."

She gazes at me. I'm sure it's a huge internal struggle, especially for someone who's lived without and worked so hard, but she knows me.

Hilda is aware that I had a spoiled upbringing and wouldn't give it to her if I didn't truly want to. Unfortunately, she knows the old Chase.

"OK, I'll accept it. Only because I can tell it's something you need to do, and your parents would be upset with me if I didn't."

I jump from my seat and hug her. I don't know where that came from, and she seems as surprised as I am. I pull away, and Hilda is crying. I've never understood this with women, but I think I made her happy.

"I can't thank you enough, Chase. You have no idea what this means for our future."

"So, you promise you won't go back to the agency? If you ever need work for some reason, you come to me."

"Yes, I promise. I'll quit today."

It worked. Skyla will be back. I leave after I get Hilda to stop crying. I never would've thought to give her the money if I didn't want to see Skyla again, but I still did the good deed, which is a start for me.

I don't know if I can get any more pathetic. I paid a hundred thousand dollars to spend only brief moments with a woman I won't give myself permission to touch.

I could have the best prostitutes on the island for less money. That's what the old me would've done with it.

Skyla

Guilt eats at me. I can't stand knowing Chase lied to the cleaning agency. I didn't earn that money, and I'm not about to take it for nothing. I'm off today, but I decide to go to Chase's to clean. If he isn't there, then I'll wait for him.

Yes, there's a part of me looking for an excuse to see him, but at least I have a legitimate one. With my cleaning supplies in hand and a magazine, I head out the door.

Chase doesn't answer when I knock. I debate on using the key, but since I'm not supposed to be in the house today, I decide against it and walk around to the back. I sit on the bottom of his steps that lead up to his patio.

At least I'll get to enjoy part of my day relaxing by the ocean in between checking for Chase's arrival back home.

Another reason I return is for the victory. He's already ordered me around enough times, so he isn't winning the next battle. I *will* be cleaning today.

"Skyla."

I look to my right and see Eric walking toward me.

"Hi."

"What are you doing on Chase's steps?" he asks.

"I'm waiting for him to come home. I didn't get to clean the other day, so I'm going to do it today."

"Good luck with that. If he doesn't know, he won't like you springing this on him."

I frown. "Is he always so overbearing? He's not going to keep ordering me around." I probably shouldn't have said that to his friend, but Chase needs to get over himself.

Eric laughs. "Yes, he is, and I might have to witness this verbal exchange. How's your arm healing?"

"It's healing nicely. It isn't that bad of a cut, so that's why I'm back. I need to do my job."

Eric studies me nervously, obvious from his fidgeting. "Skyla, would you want to get some dinner with me?"

Wow, I didn't expect that. Chase is the only man I've thought about for the last couple of days, but he's shown zero interest in me, and I'm lonely.

My brother was shipped off to Afghanistan almost as soon as I got off the plane three months ago.

"Sure, that'd be nice."

His face lights up. It definitely won't pain me to stare at those blue eyes for a couple of hours.

"OK, great. Is tonight too soon?"

"No, would seven work?"

"Yeah, um, I don't have anything to write down your address and phone number."

He's right about that. All he has with him is a surfboard and the swim trunks he's wearing.

"How about I leave it with Chase?"

"Um, I guess that'll work." Eric glances away from me. He doesn't seem too hip on that idea. What is it with Chase? It's as if he can't be disturbed.

"Well, don't let me keep you from your surfing."

He gives me a warm smile. "Talking to you is just as enjoyable, but I'll leave you alone. I'll call you after I get your number."

"See you tonight, Eric."

Rejection and Drive

Chase

I get home around eleven and remember Eric's going to be over to surf. Looking out the back windows of my home, I think of Skyla saying she'd never take the view of the ocean for granted. I soak it in a little longer for her.

After spotting Eric, I walk outside to go down to the beach. I reach the top of the stairs and freeze. She's sitting on my bottom step.

I know I just paid a hundred grand to see Skyla again, but I thought I'd have to wait until she walks the beach or comes next week to clean.

"Hi," I say.

She turns her body half way around and looks up at me. "Hi, Chase."

"What are you doing here?" I try not to sound cold, but it comes out that way.

"I was waiting for you, so I can clean."

"That's not necessary. You can do it next week."

"Next week?"

Oh, shit. She doesn't know about that. "I mean, whoever comes next week. It'll be fine until then."

"No, I can't stand that you told the agency I did the work when I didn't, so I'm staying."

"Oh, really?" I can't help smirking. She obviously doesn't know me, or she wouldn't be giving me this much attitude. Maybe I like her because she doesn't mind dishing it out. She's exciting.

"Yes, really," she says, smiling and walking up the stairs until she's one step below me. She gazes up at me with determination.

Looking at her, all I see is blue. There is the blue ocean behind her, blue sky above, and those mesmerizing blue eyes I can't help but get lost in.

"Well, are you only going to look at me, or can I get past you to work? I could use a glass of water, too. I've gotten hot sitting out here."

Dammit, how long was I staring at her? I barely move over and hold my arm up toward the house, signaling her to walk past me.

There isn't much room, so I feel her arm brush against my chest as she passes, and I want to pull her against me.

Following her into the kitchen, I fix her a glass of water. Leaning back against the kitchen counter, I cross my arms and watch her.

She quickly drinks it, staring straight into my eyes the entire time. She's different today, feistier, and I like it. Where's this coming from? She sits the glass down.

"Thanks for the water."

"No problem. You can help yourself anytime. How's the arm?"

"It's healing well. I better get to work."

Her perfect little ass sways as she walks out of my kitchen, and I watch it until she's out of my sight. She's wearing black shorts and a snug, white tank top.

Those shorts hug her ass just right, and I've paid to be tortured on a weekly basis. I have to get out of this house before I attack her.

Eric comes out of the water and walks my way as I sit on my patio. "So, is she still here, or did you make her leave?"

"If you're referring to Skyla, then she's still here."

He chuckles. I'm curious as to why this is funny, and I'm sure he's about to share.

"She won. Interesting."

"What are you getting at, Eric?"

"All I'm saying is you didn't get your way."

"I could've, but I didn't see the point. It's her job, and she's easy on the eyes, so why should I?"

"She sure is. She's gorgeous."

My jaw tightens before the rest of my body tenses up. "I'm going to go fix some lunch." I get up from my chair. I don't want to look at him right now, and I don't want him anywhere near Skyla.

"Alright, dude. I'm gonna surf, but I'll be back."

Rummaging through the fridge, I find everything needed to make a salad. I sauté some chicken strips to add to it and put them in a bowl.

Cut up pineapple goes on the table along with a few different salad dressings. Maybe if I can get Skyla to spend time with me, she'll stay away from Eric.

Skyla

I clean one of the upstairs bathrooms off of a guest room. It's been used recently, and I figure it's a friend who slept over.

I'm certain a woman would've been in his bed. I feel a tinge of jealousy toward any female who gets to be pressed against that fine body.

I hear someone coming. Determined not to be startled again, I glance toward the door. Mr. Mysterious is looking at me, and he is divine.

"Hi," he says.

"Hi. I wised up on using the iPod when cleaning the tubs, so I heard you coming."

"Um ... I made some lunch. It's hard to cook for one, so I always have too much. Would you want to join me?"

I thought Eric's request was a surprise, but this is over the top shocking. I'm starving, and I can't bring myself to turn Chase down when he asked so nicely.

Spending time with him is what I want, but that scares me. I don't need anyone to tell me he could break my heart. I'm fully aware.

"OK, if you're sure," I say politely. He flashes me a smile. I can't believe it. I thought I saw the start of one on the steps, but this is a sure thing. I wash my hands in the sink before I follow him downstairs.

Everything is displayed neatly on the table.

"Did you do all of this?"

"Yes."

"It looks delicious. Thank you."

I don't understand how someone this attractive and wealthy can be nervous. One minute he seems confident, and the next minute he acts like a scared boy.

"Sit, help yourself." He leans against the counter and watches me.

After sitting, I fix my plate. "You're going to eat with me, right?"

I'll refuse to eat if he doesn't. Hesitantly, he takes a seat and puts food on his plate. I hate feeling like I have a disease around this man.

"Have you always lived on Oahu?" I ask.

"Yes."

One word is all he offers up, but I feel his eyes on me. I'm not talking again until he speaks. Several minutes pass, and with every second of silence, I'm becoming more uncomfortable.

"I'm sorry, I can't eat with you," he says before he gets up and drops his plate hard on the counter. He goes out the glass door to his patio, leaving me sitting at his table. I'm once again humiliated.

After rinsing my plate off in the sink, I hurry back to the restroom to finish cleaning. Looking in the mirror,

I see that I'm beet red. The anger from his rejection spreads through me, fueling my energy.

Finishing up as quickly as possible, I go to my purse that's sitting on the kitchen counter. The food is put away, and I don't see or hear Chase.

I root for a pen and a piece of paper in my purse. On the back of a grocery receipt, I write a note to Eric, giving him my address and phone number.

I also add that I'm looking forward to our date. Folded, I write his name on the front and leave it on the island, so he won't miss it. Take that Mr. Moody ass.

Chase

I hear the door slam shut. Walking through the huge, empty house, I realize I've drove away the most sweet and pleasant voice that's ever been in this place.

She thinks I didn't want to eat with her when actually, I wanted to more than anything. I just couldn't stop thinking about how I didn't deserve to.

I should've drowned in that ocean. If it'd been me instead, Bud wouldn't be wasting his life the way I am. Hearing Eric say his name the other day stunned me.

I haven't heard it in months, and the sting of it took my breath away. I miss my friend. He was one cool dude. We were fucked up idiots, but damn, we were good friends.

I'll never forget that day. Eric desperately pounding on the door and ringing the doorbell had woken me around noon.

I remember sitting up and looking at the naked woman in my bed, the residue of coke still spread across the glass on my nightstand.

Bud hadn't shown up for work. He was last seen surfing with me the night before until I left him outside while he was higher than a kite.

I had gone inside to get even more fucked up and sleep with only God knows who. I sure didn't know her name.

A search boat actually found his board later that day, and my life was forever changed. Bud was gone, and it was all my fault. I had left him on the beach.

I spot the piece of paper on the counter the second I walk into the kitchen. After seeing Eric's name on the front and reading it, I slam my fist down hard on the counter.

Fuck, I drove her right to him!

I leave it there and go outside to sit on the patio. Here comes the asshole himself.

"Hey, dude. What's up?"

"Nothing." I continue to stare at the ocean.

"Is Skyla still here?"

I take a deep breath. I don't want to punch my friend over a chick. Although, Skyla's not just any woman. "She's already gone, but she left you a note on the counter."

"Sweet," Eric says before he walks into the house. He comes back out and walks past me.

"I told you not to ask her out," I say angrily.

"And I told you I was going to. I won't if you want to go out with her. Will you ask her?"

I don't answer. I can't ask her out.

"That's what I thought," he says, shaking his head as he walks down the stairs. Unless I'm going to ask her out, I can't say a damn thing to him, and he knows it.

Friend or Enemy

Skyla

Eric calls me at six to be sure we're still on for our date. I have no idea where we're going, and I don't care. It's going to be nice to have some company with someone who acts like they give a shit.

My strapless, hot pink sundress reaches mid-thigh. It's revealing but not over the top. I hear the doorbell ring right after I slip on my heels.

"Hi." I give Eric a warm smile.

"Hi, Skyla. Damn, you look great. Your hair down is beautiful."

"Thank you." We walk to his car, and he opens the door for me. He mostly asks about my job on the way to dinner, and he seems nervous. I am, too, since I haven't been on a date in almost a year. He parks at Haleiwa Joe's, a seafood restaurant.

"Have you eaten here before?" Eric asks.

"No, but I've wanted to try it."

He smiles before his hand goes to the small of my back as we stroll inside. "Good. I think you'll like it."

"How long have you lived here?" he asks after we place our orders.

"I moved here three months ago to be near my brother, Lee, but he was deployed right after I arrived.

I'd already given my notice at my place in California, and my airline tickets were already purchased, so I decided to go ahead and come."

I sure as hell didn't know it was going to be this hard to live here alone. I try to hide my sadness as I recall all the loss I've experienced in my life. Having no family around sucks.

"How about you?"

"I grew up here. My dad took a corporate job in Waikiki when I was a baby and moved us here from Nevada. I run a real estate firm. I have a lot of flexibility with my job, so I get to surf a lot."

A cheesy smile spreads across his handsome face. Surfing is obviously his first love.

"How did you meet Chase?" I'm determined to get some answers whether Chase is the one to give them to me or not.

"Our dads did business together when we were young, so we were around each other a lot. Once we could drive, we became really close. He'd either stay in Waikiki with me, or I'd stay up here, depending on where the surf was good.

"I finally moved to the North Shore a few years ago and started my real estate business. We're both twenty-five, so we've been friends for like twenty years.

"Wow, I didn't realize we've been friends that long. Chase owns a lot of property on the island going many generations back. That's where his wealth comes from. Why do you ask?"

"He's not very friendly. He acts like he wants to speak to me one minute and not the next. He did something today that hurt my feelings."

"He has some issues. He's been through some shit this year, and I'm sure he'd prefer it if I didn't share."

I sit quiet, twirling my fork on my plate. I think of all the different things it could be. Maybe someone died, or he got a divorce and had his heart broken, so he hates women. Eric chuckles, so I look up at him and see he's shaking his head.

"You already like him."

"No I don't," I snap. "That's a bold thing to say when you barely know me, don't you think?"

"Sorry. I told you about my honesty. It's good or bad depending on the topic. I guess this time it's bad."

"Chase's silence is annoying and intriguing is all. He saved my ass at the beach the other night. Some guys cornered me. I think one of their names was Troy.

"I was terrified. He ran them off and walked me home. He barely spoke, other than when he scolded me like a child for walking on the beach alone in the dark." I frown, recalling his rejection again.

"Chase did that, huh? I know Troy and his friends. I'm not sure what would've happened there. I think Troy's more talk than anything."

Eric is quiet the rest of our meal. I'm quickly seeing that asking about Chase on a date was a bad idea. He's his friend, so I don't see what the big deal is, but I'm regretting it.

Happy go lucky Eric wasn't around on the ride home, either. He parks in front of my house and looks over at me.

"Look, Skyla, I think you're attractive and sweet, but I believe I need to bow out."

"Bow out of what?" This is the strangest date I've ever been on.

"I won't compete with Chase for a woman, and I can see that he's gotten under your skin. I actually hope he shows you that he likes you. He told me not to take you out. I should've realized then how much he liked you."

"He said that?" I ask, sounding surprised.

"Yes. He seemed rather angry at me, actually. I've already seen him more alive in the last few days than I have in months.

"I need him to be happy again, so if there's a chance you could make that happen, then I'm not about to interfere. He's too good a friend. Not to mention, he'd be miserable to be around if we dated when he likes you."

I tap my fingertips on my knee. I'm not quite sure how to respond. Hearing that Chase told him not to take me out is having an effect on me. I can't deny it.

"You're an incredible friend to him. I think you're great, and I wanted to see what would happen if we went out, but hearing what Chase said did stir up some feelings. You're sweet, funny and good-looking. I wanted our date to go good."

"Chase is those things. They're just buried right now. Well, he's a dude, so I'm not going to say he's good-looking, but women seem to think so."

Eric gives me a really cute chuckle and smile. "Please be patient and give him a chance. He's a great guy."

"I can pay you for dinner. It doesn't seem fair."

"Stop. I'd like us to be friends, and there's nothing wrong with treating a friend to dinner," Eric says, squeezing my knee lightly.

"I'd really like us to be friends, too. Mahalo, Eric."

His eyes light up. "You're welcome. See, you're quickly becoming an islander."

I give him a kiss on the cheek and get out of the car.

Chase

Screw this!

I get out of bed at six in the morning after tossing and turning all night from the jealousy coursing through my veins. All I can think about is Eric and Skyla laughing and smiling.

I should've stopped him. I'll hurt him if he kissed her. Needing to release some anger, I decide to go for a run along the beach.

Skyla comes to this stretch of beach at least four times a week. I've watched her from my back steps for three months and worry every time about her safety.

She sits and gazes at the water before she plays in the sand like a child. I often see her toned thighs as her sundress blows in the wind. Her beauty drives me crazy.

She always stops as she walks, digging her toes into the sand, looking at it as if she's having a deep, unspoken conversation with it.

Screw a penny for her thoughts; I'd give her a thousand bucks to know what she thinks about that damn sand. She intrigued me before I met her, and now, I can't get enough of her.

Fuck, what is she doing to me?

After I walk home and make some coffee, I go back out onto the patio and take a seat. I spot Eric coming around the side of my house. He always parks in my drive when he comes to surf. I'm sure he wants to rub it in about his date.

"Hey, bro," Eric says as he climbs the steps.

"I made coffee if you want some." I can't look at him.

"Thanks, I'll be back." He props his board against the stairs. He comes back out with his coffee and sits in the chair next to me.

"I wanted to get a surf in and talk to you before I head home. I have some properties to show later. Um, I took Skyla out last night."

Bastard. He's not wasting any time, but I try to stay cool since he's a good friend. "How'd that work out?"

"Not so good. She's interested in someone else."

Dammit. A situation I can't control whatsoever.

"She actually told you this? Seems like she would've turned you down on the date and not wasted your time." I can see out of the corner of my eye that Eric's staring at me. I finally look over at him.

"She likes you, man," he says.

I turn my head away from him. I don't want him to see the effect his words have on me. That's not what I was expecting to hear.

"What are you talking about?"

"She kept asking about you during dinner. She's irritated at your behavior toward her, but she definitely likes you, so I'm not going to ask her out again.

"She's awesome, so I'm going to be pissed if you don't act on it. I know you like her, or you wouldn't have told me not to go out with her."

"I don't deserve to be with her. She's better than any woman I've been around."

"You're being a chicken shit, Chase. You're afraid to live. You don't have experience doing it without numbing yourself with drugs and alcohol first."

"You're right. I don't, so I need to leave this alone. I'm sure I'd somehow hurt her."

"Stop making excuses. All of your friends are sick of it, and you're not going to have any left if you don't stop wallowing in self-pity. Bud wouldn't want this, and you know it. He'd smack you upside the head right now, letting a fine piece of ass like her walk away."

I glare at him. I've thought about her that way, but I don't like hearing it out of his mouth.

"I'm playing, dude. She's a sweet girl. I wanted to see if I got a reaction out of you and I did. Ask her out. She told me you rescued her. That speaks volumes of how you've changed because you would've been too strung out to even notice her before."

"I'll think about it."

"Think about getting your ass back on that board, too. I miss having you out there. Enough of this girly talk. I'm going to catch some waves."

Anyone who's willing to walk away from a woman that amazing so my pathetic ass can have a shot with her is a good friend.

Little did Eric know, if he hadn't voluntarily given up Skyla, I was going to offer him a hundred thousand dollars to walk away from her.

Skyla

It's seven in the morning on Saturday. I sit on my couch, trying to make sense of what just happened. The cleaning agency called and told me they are permanently assigning me to Chase's home. They said he told them I did a great job.

Did he honestly fire the other lady, so I can go there and be humiliated week after week? Half of me is doing cartwheels, and the other half is angry.

I'll be relieved when I can quit this job. I get to in less than two months. That's when I turn twenty-one and receive my trust fund from my father's death.

It's been two days since my date with Eric and since I've seen Chase. It's going to be a long day now that the agency woke me up early. I'm messing with my phone when I get an idea.

I want to get to know Eric and Andy better. I need friends, and I would feel safer on this island if I had a male friend. He told me he surfs early on the weekends, so I pray I don't wake him as I dial his number.

It goes to voicemail, so I leave him a message, telling him I'd like to bring them lunch on the beach. This would ease my guilt over our date.

Taking a chance that Eric will call back and want me there, I go ahead and drive to the grocery store. I love panini sandwiches, so when I shipped some of my things over from California, I sent my panini maker.

I purchase sourdough bread, turkey and ham, several kinds of cheeses, basil pesto and Dijon mustard.

Eric calls as I arrive back home.

"Hello."

"Hi, Skyla, it's Eric."

"Hi, are you at the beach today?"

"Yep, Andy and I are both here, and the waves are good, so we'll be here for a while."

"You have to let me bring you lunch."

"I won't turn down food. It's not like we can get anything out here."

"Will you be near Chase's house?"

"We're not far from there."

"OK, I'll be there in a couple of hours. I have a hot pink bikini, so you should be able to spot me."

"I seriously doubt I could miss you, Skyla. You're one smokin' hot chick."

I giggle from his unexpected compliment.

"Um, thank you. I'll see you then."

Close to two hours later, I'm ready for the beach. After packing the sandwiches in a basket and everything else in my swim bag, I start walking and soon realize I underestimated the heaviness of what I'm carrying.

Standing back on the beach, I search the water and see who I think are Eric and Andy surfing. I watch them briefly before I go to find a spot, stopping when I see Chase sitting in a lounge chair.

His back is to me, but I can't miss his hair or build. My heart pounds as I make the realization that I have no choice but to go to him.

No matter how rude he's been to me, I can't bring myself to make things awkward for Eric and Andy by setting up away from Chase.

I can't find it in my heart to exclude him, anyway. I decide that this lunch will either make or break my attraction to him. I take a deep breath and continue walking.

The Rubdown

Chase

"Hi, Chase."

I feel the hair on my skin rise the second I hear her sweet voice. I look up, and I'm in shock that she's here and speaking to me.

"Um, hi, Skyla."

"I told Eric I'd bring him and Andy some lunch. I hope you don't mind that I'm here. I have enough food for you, too."

She's so damn adorable. I have to apologize.

"Stay here. I promise I won't bite."

She props her shades on top of her head and smiles at me. I try not to get lost once again in her captivating blue eyes. "Um, Skyla, I'm sorry about the other day when I walked out at lunch. I was dealing with some shit, and I had to get away. It wasn't personal."

Her surprised expression at my apology tells me she thinks even less of me than I thought. I watch her set her stuff down, and as she leans over to dig a towel out of her bag, I get an awesome cleavage shot. Swallowing hard, I look back up before she sees me.

"Thanks for apologizing."

She pulls her bathing suit cover off over her head and smiles at me bashfully before sitting down.

"I told Eric he could spot me by my bright bikini."

Fuck. Me. Her body is sensational.

I quickly turn my head to the ocean. I don't know how I'm going to stay out here with her, but if I leave now, she'll never speak to me again, and there's no way I'm leaving her alone with the guys.

I don't even want them to see her body, and why is she here to see them, anyway? I don't know how I'm going to keep my eyes from wandering down her sexy, flawless skin.

"I ... I want to ask you something before your friends come over here. I'll be embarrassed if I'm wrong, but did you fire your housekeeper?"

She looks out toward the water and picks at her towel. I never considered her asking me about Hilda.

"I didn't have her fired. She quit; however, I did ask them to send you to replace her."

She looks back at me. "OK. I don't know why you would do that, but thanks. I'll try my best to tolerate your home and the breathtaking view of the ocean it offers," she says jokingly.

I see Eric and Andy coming toward us. I wish they'd stay the hell away.

"You're right. The bikini is hard to miss, and so is the hot babe in it," Eric says.

Skyla blushes. I want to punch him in the face. I watch them both scan her body with their greedy eyes.

"Aloha, Skyla," Andy says.

"Aloha, Andy. Thanks, Eric. You're a flirt, but I can't say I mind the compliments," she says.

"It's firing today," Eric says enthusiastically.

"Chase, did you see that big turn I threw down?" Andy asks.

"No, sorry, I was talking to Skyla."

"I brought food, but I don't know if you'll like it. I love to make panini sandwiches, so I brought several different kinds. I also have soft drinks, water and chips."

She slips her bathing suit cover back on before she starts getting the food out. I'm relieved. I'm also wondering if Eric asked her out again. I'll have to hurt him if he's changed his mind about pursuing her.

"You didn't have to do all this, Skyla," he says.

"That's what friends do, and we're friends now, remember? I owe you after the other night."

She flashes Eric a wide grin. I want to make her smile like that.

Andy lightly squeezes her arm. "Thanks for the food, Skyla."

I wish I could tell them to keep their damn hands off of her. She's mine. I didn't pay a hundred thousand dollars for them to eat her food and eye fuck her.

"You're welcome. Chase, please eat with us."

I can't turn her down. She's like sunshine today.

"Give me whichever sandwich you think is the best."

"This is my favorite. It's turkey with provolone and basil pesto." She hands it to me on a paper plate, and our fingers meet underneath. The touch of her fingers is the kindling to the fire.

"Now, this is a moment when I want you to use Eric's blunt honesty skills. You need to tell me if you don't like it. I'll just eat that one if you don't," she says, gazing up at me from her towel with a smile. I take a bite of the sandwich, and it's really good.

"The sandwich tastes great, Skyla." A huge grin spreads across her face, and it warms me knowing I put it there.

"Thanks, I figure it's something different. I love this panini place in California."

"Are you from there?" I ask her.

"Yes, I moved here three months ago. My brother is stationed here in the Army, but he's deployed to Afghanistan."

Oh, no. Her smile disappears, and I've caused that.

"I've been to California quite a few times. My mom is from San Diego. My dad met her while on vacation there."

"That's where I'm from," she says cheerfully. "It's about as close as you're going to get to Hawaii weather." Her smile returns.

"Oh, nice barrel, Eric," she says. "I saw it when I was walking up. The swell looks pretty solid. I've always heard about the waves on the North Shore, but you have to see it to fully understand." All of our eyes flash to her.

"Do you surf, Skyla?" Eric asks.

"Yes."

"Why is your ass not out there? It's almost November. We're getting into the best time to surf here," he says.

"I haven't surfed for months. I—I haven't wanted to be on my board. I'm hopeful that I'll want to soon."

"You're going to have to show us your skills," Andy says with a grin.

She surfs, and I can't believe we're both taking a break from our boards. I swear this woman was made for me, and I didn't need a reason to find her any hotter.

All of us talk surf for a while, and I'm amazed over how much she knows about it. It's obvious she's experienced.

"Thanks for lunch, Skyla. Are you ready to surf, Eric?" Andy asks.

"Sure. Talk to you later, chick. Thanks for the sandwich." Eric gives her a broad grin.

I'm glad to see he's leaving. She puts the food away and spreads her towel out. The next thing I know, she's stripping off her cover again.

Sitting next to me on her towel, I watch out of the corner of my eye as she starts rubbing sunscreen all over her body.

I have shades on, but I still close my eyes. I can't watch anymore, but I'll be taking that image to the shower with me.

"Um, Chase, would you mind putting sunscreen on my neck and back? I'd do it myself if I could. I've been getting too much sun there since I have no one to do it. I guess I need to find some girlfriends to hang out with on this island."

Shit, she wants me to rub lotion on her bare skin. I can't tell her no, and I can't deny that I want to do it.

"Sure." I try not to sound too eager as Skyla sits down in front of my chair and hands me the lotion, taking me by surprise. My chair is a low one that sits right above the sand, so her back is practically between my legs.

Since I live on the beach, I've done this for other women over the years but never have I wanted to so badly. I rub the lotion between my hands and start at her lower back.

I'll feel guilty about this later, but I'm going to stretch this out as long as I fucking can. I move slowly, massaging her skin in a circular pattern. After pouring more lotion, I work my way up her back.

"I have a hunch you've done this before. You're really good at it," she says softly.

"Um, when you live on the beach, it's a given." I continue my way up, spreading lotion out over her silky shoulders, gliding my restless hands up and down her arms. Then I move to her neck and apply the last of it before I gently massage it with my thumbs.

Swearing I hear a whimper, I want nothing more than to devour every inch of her body. I finally stop, but I don't say anything. Something is happening between us, and I'm at a loss for words.

Sitting up on her knees, she turns around to face me, now inches away from being between my legs. I've always taken what I wanted, so this is torture. It's exactly what I deserve.

Skyla gazes at me with those ocean blues, and all I can see in my head is her gazing up at me like that with her mouth around my cock.

"Thanks," she says before she stands to go back to her towel.

Stretching out on her stomach, she puts her fine ass on display, and I can't take another minute of this. If I stick around any longer, I'll say all the charming things she wants to hear. Then if I'm lucky, she'll be mine, and that can't happen.

"I have to go, Skyla, but thanks for lunch. It's been cool hanging out with you."

Rolling over onto her back, she looks up at me through her sunglasses. God, I'd love to pounce on her. She covers her forehead with her hand, shielding her face from the sun.

"Can I ask why you're not surfing?"

"I'm taking a break from my board, too." I look out at the ocean. I don't want her to see me weak and broken.

"I'm sorry, I should mind my own business. I hope the rest of your day is good."

"I'm certain I've already experienced the best part of it, Skyla. I'll see you Tuesday." I turn and walk away, stunned that I shared that with her.

A Second Chance

Skyla

I wish he'd stay with me and talk. What is he hiding? He said the sweetest words, and damn it felt incredible when he touched me.

I didn't want him to stop, and I don't think he wanted to. I'm in big trouble. I don't know how I'll keep him out of my head.

"You're going to fry out here."

Eric's standing over me, letting water fall onto my body, and it feels good after lying in the sun.

"Are you leaving?" I ask.

"Yeah, I've been out a long time today. I need a nap." His blue eyes glisten as he smiles at me. He's eyeing my body, so I decide to sit up, and he plops down in the sand next to me. "I see Chase went home."

"He did. I still can't figure him out, but at least he was nice to me today. He's a man of few words, that's for sure."

"He used to not shut up. I can tell he likes you, but if you tell him I talk to you about this stuff, I'll deny it. Then, the next time you're out here, I'll toss your cute ass in the ocean."

"Will you be out here next weekend? If so, I'll bring lunch again."

"Probably, but I'll call to let you know. You can't spoil me, or I might have to tell Chase to take a hike."

I push his shoulder with my hand, and he almost falls over before we both start laughing. I really hope we become good friends, but the flirting will have to stop. "Why don't you have a girlfriend?"

"I guess I haven't wanted to make time for one. Chicks don't exactly want a boyfriend who only works and surfs. I couldn't resist asking you out though. I've been thinking more about making time for a girlfriend."

"Well, I'm sure it won't be hard for you to find one if you can keep that filter of yours closed a little bit," I say, giggling.

"That's it girl, you're going into the ocean." Eric swiftly picks me up.

"Please, no! I'm getting ready to leave, and I'll have sand everywhere."

"OK, I guess I'll let you off the hook this time." Standing me up, he hugs me, and I imagine Chase's arms around me the entire time.

"See you later, Skyla. I know you're alone, so if you ever need anything at all, please call me."

"Thanks, Eric. That means a lot to me." I pack up my stuff and start walking home. It's been a good day, but I hate going back to an empty house.

***

It's Tuesday, so I go to Chase's. I make myself look better than I probably should for cleaning, but I can't help it. I long for him to want to spend time with me.

I'm determined to crack the code to the safe he keeps his secrets in. My stomach knots when I knock on the door.

It's not long before he opens it and gives me a friendly smile. It's not the big one I was hoping for, but I'll take it.

He looks like he just showered, and I can instantly smell his clean scent. He's so damn gorgeous in his swim trunks and tight t-shirt, and I believe he saw me ogling him.

"Hi, Chase. I imagine your house doesn't need it yet, but I have to clean on the same day every week unless you tell them not to send me."

"Come in. Just clean what you think needs it."

Immediately, he wanders off. I have no right to feel hurt, but I do. Picking the wrong guys to fall for is the norm for me. I've only had a few boyfriends, and they were losers.

Putting my earbuds in, I get to work. After thirty minutes, I'm already finished with the upstairs. I look for Chase but don't see him anywhere, so I peek out the front door and realize his car is gone.

I can't believe he left without saying a word to me. I have to get him out of my system and find someone else to be attracted to. I go into his game room that has a pool table and monstrous television.

There are surfboards hanging up on the walls, and I find myself curious again as to why he doesn't surf. After cleaning the room, I stand in front of the couch and admire the boards that are placed above it. They are top of the line.

Suddenly, I hear Chase yell my name. Alarmed, I spin around and start to fall backward. Just before I land on the couch, he grabs me and pulls me into the warm muscles of his chest.

Feeling his arms wrap around my waist, I sink against him and stand motionless for a few seconds. After breathing in the intoxicating scent on his shirt, I slowly look up at him.

He gazes down at me and smirks as he reaches a hand up and pulls out one of my earbuds.

"I think these are hazardous to your health. There's no good way to approach you with these things in."

"I'm sorry. I don't like the quiet, but I think you're right. I was admiring your boards."

My arms are pinned between our chests, and all I can think about is how I wish he'd put his free arm back around me and kiss me. His touch is like a cover, protecting me from a cool breeze.

He gently drops my earbud and wraps his arm around my waist. *Yes.* We're gazing at each other, and I realize I'm weak around this man.

He doesn't know it, and I don't understand it, but I think I'd do anything he asked.

"I came to see if you'd eat lunch with me. I promise I won't leave this time, so let me make it up to you. I already ran out to Macky's shrimp truck, and I can't eat all the food I bought."

He's still holding me, which seems odd, but I love it. I need Chase to hold on to me and never let go. My strength on this island is waning, and I realize how much I yearn for physical contact.

Eric reaching his hand out to me when I fell into the bathtub was the first physical contact I'd had in three months. That's sad. It's no wonder I want to be wrapped in Chase's arms.

"I like that place," I say with what has to be a goofy grin on my face. I'm giddy that he wasn't trying to be mean when he left me here alone.

"Come on then," he says, chuckling.

I guess I did give him a goofy grin, and I'll keep making that face if it'll keep that smile on his. I eagerly follow him into the kitchen.

Chase

Holding her in my arms felt damn good, but I shouldn't have done it. It's getting harder to resist her. Her scent is arousing, and I want to kiss her, but I know it'll open a door I can't guarantee I could close.

I held her awhile, debating. I'm challenging my demons, but they're still winning. I went out to get lunch to make up for being an ass to her last week.

We get to the kitchen, and I tell her to get the food out while I make us something to drink.

"So, you've had Macky's before. What do you think about the food trucks?"

"I find that the best food is usually where you least expect it. That was one of the first places my brother took me when I got here."

"Did you only move here to be near him?"

"Besides a few aunts, uncles and cousins, Lee is all I have for family. I got into Brigham Young for the spring semester."

"Are you Mormon?" I ask her, sounding more surprised than I should.

"No. You don't have to be to go there, but it's harder to get in. Luckily, I've always made good grades and have good test scores. I'm going to study marine biology.

"I only have to work for a couple more months until my birthday, and then I can just focus on school. Cleaning is definitely not the job I want to do forever."

She's smart. Is there anything wrong with this woman? She can't leave that soon.

"That's awesome you're going to study marine biology. Living here will be great for that."

"What do you do?" she asks.

"I lease out properties I own on the island, mostly to businesses, and a lot of them are in Waikiki. I don't have any kind of set schedule. Eric and I do a lot of work together. He finds people and businesses who are looking to lease my property. It's a win for both of us."

"Eric seems like a good friend. I really like his positive energy."

"He's been that way as long as I've known him, and he is a great friend." Where is she going with this? Does she like him? She'd be better off with him.

"Thanks for lunch. It's really good," she says, smiling as we eat.

I've never spent time with a woman who has her act together. I want every part of her. She's everything right in the world, bundled into one sweet, beautiful package.

I could look at that smile and listen to her talk for hours but I can't. The more I'm with her, the more I realize she deserves someone better.

Eric is a better man. He didn't fuck up his life and cost someone theirs. She wouldn't be sitting here talking to me if she knew about the old Chase.

I need to step aside for Eric. That would be the right thing to do, and I'm trying to be less selfish.

"Chase, are you OK?"

I snap out of my daze when I hear my name.

"Sorry, I'm fine."

"I don't have any right to know what you're thinking, but you don't have to pretend with me. It's obvious you have shit going on, and I hope whatever it is, you'll find a way to heal from it."

Did she really say that? She's mature and too open like Eric. I'm feeling extremely uncomfortable, and I can't leave. I told her I wouldn't, but all I want to do is get away from her. She's making me think of Bud.

"You should go out with Eric again. It seems you two have a lot in common, and I'm sure he'd like to."

She looks at me as if my words have crushed her.

"You want me to go out with Eric?" she asks in almost a whisper.

"I said you should."

She looks away from me and starts moving around the kitchen with urgency, cleaning up her spot at the table and clearing her plate.

"There wasn't much to clean today, so I'm going to go. Thanks for lunch."

I'm trying to do what's right, but I keep upsetting her. "I'm sorry, Skyla."

She waves her hand at me like she's swatting me away. "It's OK, I'm going. I—I get it. I'm just your housekeeper," she says as she heads for the door. It slams, and I'm left feeling like a complete asshole.

King of the Castle

Skyla

I don't know how someone can have this kind of effect on me and make me feel this humiliated. I can't continue doing this. I have to call the agency and get someone else to clean his damn home.

Chase made it quite obvious that he doesn't want me. Why can't I be attracted to Eric the way I am to Chase?

He's handsome, smart, funny and kind but no, instead, I'm screwed up in the head and only want men who need fixing.

***

After a couple of days of pouting, I go down to the beach in the evening. It's getting dark, but I don't care. Surely those same loser guys won't be there to bother me.

Wearing my white sundress, I take off my flip flops and sit down. I bury my toes in the sand as salty droplets slide along my cheeks.

I've always been strong, but the loneliness is getting to me. I might have to move back to Cali where I at least have my best friend, Brooke.

I wipe my eyes, but the tears keep coming. Pulling my knees up to my chest, I listen to the waves crashing in front of me, crashing around my world.

I feel as if I'm being tossed about in the ocean. I'm trying to find my way to shore, but with every bit of progress, another wave crashes down on me, sending me out farther.

I'm alone there, bobbing around lost. I want to swim up to the part of the shore where I belong. The place where I can stay because it has everything and everyone I need.

I want this to be that spot, but Bud will never be here again, and I need him. We grew up together and were inseparable as kids. He's my first cousin, and we lived down the street from each other growing up.

His name is Daniel, but most everyone called him Bud. He always dreamed of living in Hawaii and moved here when he turned eighteen.

When Lee joined the Army, he put in to be stationed here, so they could spend time together, and he actually got the orders. We made so many plans for what we'd do when I moved to Oahu.

Lee, Bud and I were going to have a blast. I couldn't wait to be near them again, but all those dreams were shattered when Bud died here nine months ago. Lee said he lost his life in this area.

"Skyla."

I jump and look back when I hear my name. There stands Mr. Moody, and he's scowling. What's new? I turn back toward the water.

"What are you doing out here at night again? We discussed this. Are you trying to get yourself killed?" he asks angrily.

"Go away, Chase. I can do what I please." He's exhausting.

"No, I won't go away. You obviously don't care about your safety."

"What does it matter to you?" He's not going to tell me what to do. I don't know what castle he came from, but he's not king of the beach.

"Skyla, I worry about something happening to you. You could get hurt out here this late, and why are you crying?"

I stare ahead at the darkness. Chase is one of those big waves that keeps crashing down on me.

"Go away. I can't take another second of your moody behavior. And just so you know, I won't be back to clean again. I'm not sticking around so you can make me feel like shit."

He groans loudly. I wouldn't have a clue what he's mad about since he doesn't share a damn thing. Great, he's going to sit next to me.

"Look, I don't want anyone to hurt you."

"You sure don't have an issue with hurting me."

"I never meant to hurt you, Skyla."

I see him run his hands through his hair as he slowly blows out a deep breath. "Can I ask why you're at this part of the beach again?"

"It's definitely not to get your attention. It's close to my house, and it ... it means something to me."

"This part of the beach means something to me, too," he says.

"I guess so since your backyard is the fucking ocean."

"Damn, you're really pissed at me."

"Chase, I'm a kind person, but you've managed to hurt my feelings more than once, so I'm trying to protect myself from you. It's a shame you're so closed off, and you make the choice to live this way."

"I know I do, but it's what I deserve."

I get up. I can't take his self-pity. I don't know what he's done to feel he deserves this, but I don't believe he's a bad person. I dust off the backside of my dress and start walking. He's on his feet in seconds.

"I'm walking you home."

"No, I do this all the time."

"I'm going to follow you."

I turn back around and stare at him.

"Why are you doing this to me?" I ask in desperation. Silence ... more silence. I groan with aggravation and begin to flee.

He grabs me and pulls me to his chest. One of his arms snake around my waist as the other cups the back of my head. My breath catches. I hold it in my lungs, and it feels suffocating, full of emotion needing released.

"I like you, and I don't want anything happening to you, Skyla."

He's gazing down at me, and for the first time, I feel his emotions. His heart is thundering beneath my forearm, his eyes pleading, almost desperate, and his breathing is harsh and uneven.

I can't take this. He's a virus, making every cell in my being his host. He's going to hurt me if I don't stay away from him.

"You have a weird way of showing a girl you like her, Chase. Get off of me." I jerk free of his hold as my tears defy me. I run, and I run, hearing his feet strike the pavement behind me. Once inside, I slam the door and lean up against it.

Before falling asleep, I think about how I only have two more days before I can hang out with Eric and Andy at the beach, and I hope Chase doesn't show this time.

***

I go to the grocery Saturday morning, and this time I decide to make barbecue. It's something easy for the guys to eat on the beach.

After packing up my stuff, I begin the walk, lugging my basket and swim bag again. I don't see Chase anywhere, and I have mixed feelings about that.

It's what I said I wanted, but part of me is disappointed, and I'm angry at myself for feeling this way.

I told Eric I'd have a bright green bikini on this time. I might have to buy more of them to make a game out of this. It's sad that picking which bikini to wear is the extent of the excitement in my life.

They come walking toward me with their wet, tanned bodies, sparkling eyes and ripped abs. I can't understand why these two don't have women hanging on them.

"You're awesome, Skyla. I'm starving," Andy says.

"Good, I hope you like barbecue."

Eric squeezes my shoulder as he sits down next to me. "Sounds great. I'm digging the neon green bikini. It goes good with your blonde hair."

"I think I'll keep trading you food for compliments." We sit and talk surf again. It makes me feel close to Bud, but deep down I know it won't change anything.

"Shit," Eric says.

I see that he's looking down the beach toward Chase's home. I glance that way and see him in his chair. There are two women standing in front of him talking. I thought my bikini was small until I saw theirs.

A pull of a string, and they'd be naked. They don't have a wholesome look, and that's a nice way of putting it. Jealousy hits me. He's smiling at them, and I hate it.

"Do you know those girls talking to Chase?"

"Um, those girls used to hang out with him and another friend of ours. They're trouble. Chase should have the sense to send them on their way.

"I know he hasn't seen them for a long time, so he's probably just being nice," Eric replies.

"Do you two have plans tonight?" I ask.

"I don't," Andy says.

"I don't, either. Do you have something in mind?" Eric is giving me a wide grin.

"I need some drinks, but I won't be twenty-one for almost two months. Any ideas?"

"We need to go into Waikiki. I have a friend that owns a bar there, and he'll let you in. I don't need to get busted for contributing to a minor. You're a baby, Skyla, but your body sure doesn't look like it."

"Stop, Eric. You're embarrassing me." I push him over again with my hand. "That sounds great. I told Chase last night that I'm not cleaning for him anymore.

"He's managed to treat me like crap every time I've been around him. I'm done and need a fun night out away from here."

Eric looks angry as he stares toward Chase.

"He needs to wise his ass up. He's a fool to do you that way."

"It's OK. It's not like he owes me anything. We don't even know each other. I know more about you guys than I think I ever could about him."

"I actually live farther away than Andy. Can you bring her down?" Eric asks him.

Andy looks at me and smiles. "I don't mind at all as long as you don't mind riding with me."

"Of course not. Um ... I've been wondering what you do for a career, Andy?"

"I'm an IT guy. I have the eight to five job, so that's why I don't get to surf as often as the slacker here." He smirks at Eric.

"Yeah, whatever. You're just jealous."

Andy looks back at me. "My parents were in the military and decided to live here after they got out." Standing up, he grabs his short board. "I guess we're going back in, so what if I pick you up at eight?"

"That sounds awesome." I tell him where I live and pack up my stuff. I want to stay on the beach, but I can't stand knowing Chase is that close by.

I'm sure he sees me hanging out with his friends again, and a part of me feels bad that he was left out.

What's my deal?

He's the one who's acted like a total ass for over a week. I shouldn't feel bad, but I do.

Chase

I go back up to the patio when I see Skyla leave. I know better than to get near her right now. The other night was the closest I've been to her angelic face, and it took everything in me not to taste those plump, red lips of hers.

I was an ass to grab her like that. I had no right after telling her to go out with Eric. I've been giving her mixed signals, so it's no wonder she ran from me.

"You're a dumbass," Eric says as he reaches the top of my steps.

"What are you talking about?"

"Skyla. Why would you screw that up?"

"I told you why. She's amazing and deserves someone better."

"She asked Andy and me to go out with her. I like her a lot. I'm not going to make the first move since I don't know if she still likes you, but if she shows interest in any way, then I'm jumping on the opportunity. You're right; she's fucking amazing."

"Eric, I told her to go out with you."

"Why?"

"I can't date her, and she mentioned how she digs your happy energy or some shit. Try again, OK? I want to be her friend somehow, but I'll leave her alone otherwise."

"If you're sure, bro."

Eric goes back to the beach, and I feel empty again. He's good enough for her, but I can't stand the thought of them together. I want her, and deep down I hope she won't fall for him.

Nixie

Eric

Andy shows up at Beach Surf Bar in Waikiki. He has Skyla with him who's a fox. She's in a short, silky red dress that shows her awesome legs, and her hair is down.

She gives me a cute smile as she approaches the table. Getting up, I wrap my arms around her, smelling a floral scent. "Hi, Eric," she says.

"I worried Andy might try to take you somewhere else to keep you to himself."

"I thought about it, bro. She looks mighty fine tonight." Andy smiles at Skyla.

He needs to stop flirting with her. How many guys am I going to have to compete with?

"What's going to be your drink tonight?" Andy asks her.

"I want to try a beer brewed in Hawaii."

"I got this one," he says before he goes to the bar.

Skyla and I sit down at the table. "As usual, you look incredible tonight, Skyla."

"Thanks, Eric. I'm going to be expecting these compliments every time I see you if you don't stop it."

"Don't worry, I'll keep giving them." I wink at her and squeeze her hand. I need to find out tonight if she still has feelings for Chase. Andy brings us our beers. She tries hers and loves it. I have a feeling from her lively mood that she plans on drinking a lot of them.

A few of my other friends show up, and two of them have their girlfriends with them. You'd think Skyla's never seen another female before. She immediately starts talking to the women and wins them over easily.

I'm thankful they're here. They'll dance with her. I want no part of that and neither does Andy. The poor girl is starved for attention, and I hate that she's been alone for so long.

I lose track of Skyla's beers after the third. The drunker she gets, the more often she comes over and asks me about Chase. I'm either answering her questions about him or trying to keep men off of her. This sucks.

"Do you think Chase really likes me?"

"I think so, Skyla," I reply pissed.

"Why won't he show me?"

This goes on for a couple of hours between dancing with her new girlfriends and other men. We already covered on our first date that she likes Chase. I'm disappointed, but I should've never expected different from her.

Chase telling us to go out with each other isn't going to magically change her feelings. Finally, she comes over and sits with Andy and me. She's hammered and giggling like a teenage girl.

"Hi, guys. I've had fun. Thanks for bringing me out."

"You're welcome, Skyla. You're entertaining," Andy says.

"It's nice to talk to some females. I miss my girlfriends. I've never had very many. I grew up with guys, so I get along better with them."

"It didn't look like you were having any trouble winning over my buddies' girls," I say.

"I need some girlfriends here. I was supposed to spend my time on this island with my cousin and brother, but my cousin died nine months ago, and then you know about Lee being deployed. That just left little ol' me."

In an instant, her demeanor changes. She appears upset and gazes out toward the dance floor.

"Skyla, are you OK?" I ask.

She gives me a faint smile. "I'm sorry. I miss Bud. I'm not trying to bring you down, so I'll shut up about it. Let's talk about something else."

I hold my breath. She said her cousin died here nine months ago, and his name is Bud.

No fucking way!

I look over, and Andy's eyes are wide and locked on mine.

"Skyla, if you need to talk about it, it's OK. Who was your cousin again?"

"His name is Bud. We were really close. He disappeared one night when he was surfing. He lived on the North Shore, too."

I swallow hard. Andy coughs and looks like he's choking before he quickly stands.

"I think we need more beers," he says.

He wants any reason to get away from this damn table, and if he hadn't, I would've. This could send Chase over the deep end. It could really kill him, and I can't lose another friend.

"Why haven't you said anything before now, Skyla?"

"I don't like to talk about it. Well, I guess until tonight, and it's probably because I'm drunk." She puts her arms on the table and rests her head on them.

I'm freaking out! I have no clue what to do with this information. None of us flew to California for the memorial service. We decided to have our own service here, so we could stay close to Chase.

He was a fucking mess. If one of us had gone, then we would've met Skyla, and I wouldn't be having a coronary at the moment. I've got to talk to Andy.

"Skyla, your new girlfriends are dancing. Why don't you go out there and dance some more. It might make you feel better."

Andy comes back with our beers. "Here, Skyla. I got you another beer."

She perks up after she takes a couple of drinks.

"You're right. I don't want to ruin our night talking about depressing stuff. I'll go dance."

"What the hell, Eric?" Andy's flipping out as soon as she stumbles away. "What are we going to do? We can't tell Chase, but it's only a matter of time before she mentions Bud in front of him."

"I know. I can't believe this is happening. Oh my god, she's Nixie, and she's Rock's baby sister. I'm guessing his real name is Lee. He'd kill us right now if he knew we got her drunk at a bar. Why in the hell did Bud call him Rock?"

"I believe it had something to do with him throwing rocks at all the kids in the neighborhood. Bud's hot cousin from California is really here, and he was damn right about the 'hot' part.

"Why'd he have to give everyone he knows nicknames? That's why she doesn't know who we are. If Bud ever mentioned us, he would've only used our nicknames," Andy says.

I run my hands through my hair. "And if Chase hadn't made us stop using them, then we wouldn't be dealing with this shit right now.

"Bud said she was moving here, but he said it for so long that I didn't believe him, and after he died, I never thought about it again.

"This is going to stir up all the shit we've been trying to get past. I miss him bad, and knowing who she is makes me feel like he's here, man."

"What do we do?" Andy asks with desperation in his voice.

"Look, we can't tell her or Chase. He's all she's talked about tonight. I was hoping to have a shot with her, but she wants to be with him, and I know he likes her. We have to hope they fall in love fast."

"How is the two of them falling in love going to help this?"

"If they fall for each other before they make the connection, maybe their relationship can survive it. Chase has been happier since he met her.

"It's almost like it's meant to be. Do you remember how Bud always joked about fixing Chase up with his Nixie? It's what he wanted."

Andy looks at me with so much sadness in his eyes, and I want to fucking scream at the top of my lungs for our good friend dying.

"I remember," he says.

Andy and I start drinking even heavier, trying to numb the pain that's been brought to the surface.

Another hour passes, and I realize there's no way any of us can drive home.

"I have to call Chase to come get us," I say.

"No way!"

"We have to. She's totally wasted, and neither of us can drive. It's actually the perfect time to put her near Chase. He'll take care of her, and it might bring them together."

Andy runs his hands down his face.

"Fine, but you better hope this works."

Angel of Temptation

Chase

It's about midnight when my cell rings.

"Cuz, what are you doing?" Eric asks.

"What do you think? I'm going to bed."

"I need your help. Andy drove Skyla here to Beach Surf in Waikiki. He wasn't going to drink much, but damn she can put the beer away, so we kept drinking with her. There's no way any of us can drive home. Could you come get us?"

"Dammit, why'd you take her all the way there?"

"She's only twenty, and she told me she wanted to go drinking. I couldn't take her anywhere else."

"I didn't know she was that young. Are you trying to get your ass thrown in jail? You better keep her safe."

The whole time I'm talking to him, I'm getting dressed and finding my keys. "I swear I'll hurt you bad if anything happens to her."

"We got carried away. She's cool to hang out with, but I might have to kick someone's ass. The men in here won't leave her the hell alone."

"Shit, I'm leaving now." I can't drive fast enough. The thought of other men groping her has me pissed off. If something happens to someone else I care about, I'm done.

Since it's late, and I'm breaking the law, I shave an hour drive down to almost thirty minutes. I haven't stepped foot into a bar in nine months, so that's adding to my anxiety.

I see Skyla dancing with Eric when I walk in. He has her pulled right up against his chest, and I see them talking before she kisses his damn cheek. I want to vomit. I've already lost her when she should be with me. I tap on his shoulder. "Eric."

He pulls away from Skyla some but still holds on to her. Her glazed eyes lock with mine, and she smiles.

"Chase, did you drive all the way here to dance with me? If so, that is super sweet and not like the asshole you normally are."

"Real nice. I'm here ten seconds, and I'm already an asshole."

"Don't act like one if you don't want to be called one," she says, giggling.

"Find Andy and meet me at the car," I say angrily to Eric as I grab Skyla's hand. I start walking and quickly realize that Eric had to have been holding her up when they were dancing.

She's practically falling on her face. I grab her and hold her against me until we get to the car.

"I should've known you didn't want to dance with me," she says, poking me in the chest.

"Please tell me you're not going to throw up in my vehicle."

"If you're nice to me, I won't." Her speech is slurred, and it's already hard to decipher between her giggling. I want to be mad at her for endangering herself again, but her giggling is cute, so she's making it difficult.

I help her into the passenger seat and get in the car. Reaching right over, she rubs the back of my hair.

"Chase, you have the best hair. It's silky soft. I've wanted to touch it since I met you."

I pull her hand down and hold it between our seats. She jerks it away from me. "Why don't you like me?"

"I do like you, but we need to only be friends. Eric likes you, so you should be thrilled about that."

"I'd be *thrilled* if you liked me, but you have a sucky way of showing a woman you care."

"I'm trying not to show you."

"Well, that's mean. Why?" Her hand finds its way back into my hair. This is torture.

"You deserve better than a guy like me."

"I should get to be the judge of that, not you."

I see Eric and Andy walking to the car, so I pull her hand back down and place it in her lap.

"You're so mean to me, Chase. I'm trying to get over you." She's gazing at me with half open eyes and can barely get her words out.

Keeping her from touching me on our way to Eric's is a challenge, and I imagine he's noticing. This situation with the three of us is getting uncomfortable.

I park in his driveway and go around to the passenger side to help him with Skyla, but before I can open her door, Eric puts his hand out in front of me.

"Don't, man."

"Don't you want her to stay with you? You can take her home in the morning when you're sober."

"She doesn't want to be with me, Chase. I'm done trying. We're only going to be friends."

"I saw you two dancing, and I saw her kiss you."

"As soon as she had some alcohol in her, I had to hear your name a million times. She kissed my cheek after she told me what a good friend I am. I'm not getting out of the friend zone, so you need to quit being stupid and date her."

"We've talked about this already."

"Yeah, and I know you want to, so stop being an ass. Look, I'm worried about her being alone tonight. She might get sick. Can you take her back to your place without touching her?"

He has a lot of nerve saying that to me when his hands were all over her. "I'll take her to my place, and don't worry, I'm not going to doing anything with her. I sure can't say the thought isn't there, but I won't."

Eric points at me. "Keep your damn hands off of her unless you're dating her."

I yank his finger down from the front of my face.

"You're drunk, Eric. Shut the hell up and get into the house."

"Alright, alright, I'm going."

After I see Eric open his front door, we leave. I keep having to remove her hand from my hair. She has my dick hard, and I'm seriously thinking about fucking her in this damn car after I drop Andy off if she doesn't cut this shit out.

Andy lives close to me, so I drop him off and drive to my house. Skyla's looking sleepy when we get there, so I decide it's easier to pick her up and carry her inside.

"You're strong, Chase, and your muscles are impressive." Her arms are around my neck, and she's giving me a provocative look as I take the stairs up to the bedrooms.

"Thanks, Skyla." The second I lay her on the bed, she grabs my shirt and pulls me down on top of her. I want to kiss her more than anything, so I quickly stand back up.

"Why did you bring me here if you don't plan on taking advantage of me? Right now, I really want you to. It's been way too long since I've had sex, and I bet you're really good at it."

I swear I want to taste her and touch her.

"Dammit, Skyla, nothing can ever happen between us, so stop saying shit like that." She's inviting, sprawled out on the bed, so I run my hand through my hair.

The idea of messing around with her keeps running through my head, but I'm scum if I do something with her right now, especially when I'm sober.

"Why do you have to be such an ass? I like you. I can't even get you to touch me when I'm throwing myself at you.

"Can you at least sleep next to me? I promise I won't take advantage of you." She giggles before her expression changes, and now she appears sad.

"Please, Chase. I've lost almost every person who means something to me. I'm lonely."

God, I could make her feel better, and I hate thinking she's carrying pain with her. I know how that feels. "I'm going to get you some water. Can you stay awake that long?"

"Yes, I'll do that." Her eyes close, and I figure she'll be out before I ever get back to the room. I go downstairs to fix her a glass of water.

Fuck, when I return, she's lying on the bed in nothing but her bra and panties. I look around and find her dress on the floor.

I've already seen her in a bikini, but there's something about seeing her in a silky, black bra and panties that sets me on fire.

I roll her over, so I can get the blankets out from underneath her. I get her under the covers, strip down to my boxers and get into bed with her.

I've never slept next to a woman that I didn't have sex with first. I shouldn't do this for both our sakes, but she never threw up, and I'm worried she might in her sleep.

If she's pissed at me in the morning for sleeping in the bed with her, that's my story. I am actually worried about her. I never thought I'd care about protecting someone this much.

I lie facing her and stroke her hair. She scoots her body up against me, burying her face into my chest. I wrap my arms around her, and for the first time in my life, I want to cuddle. I never want to forget how good she feels.

I don't know how long I'll be able to resist you, angel.

Skyla

I wake up to warmth. I'm snuggled up to something, and it feels great. My eyes flash open, and I'm staring at skin, so I jerk back and realize I'm in bed with Chase.

Shit, shit, shit!

The events from the night before rush back to me, except I can't remember coming into this room. I feel exposed, so I lift up the sheet and peek under, finding that I'm only in my bra and panties.

Did I have sex with him? There's no way. I'd most certainly remember. I've fantasized about it enough times to know I wouldn't forget something like that.

As I stare at Chase's dark skin and his smooth, firm bicep that's resting outside of the sheet, I wonder why he's in the guest bed with me. I quietly get up and walk to the restroom.

He's staring at me when I come out. Play it cool, Skyla. After swiftly walking to the bed, I pick up my dress and pull it over my head.

"Good morning," he says.

"I don't know if I'd say that. I feel awful."

"I bet."

"I'm sorry you had to come get us. Did you remove my dress?" I sit on the side of the bed and gaze at him.

"I went to get you some water, and when I came back, you'd taken it off and thrown it on the floor."

"Why did you sleep in bed with me?"

"You asked me to. You didn't want to be alone, and I was worried you might get sick."

"This is embarrassing." I lay my face in my hands as my elbows rest on my legs.

"You were funny. For the most part, you're a happy drunk."

"Thanks for picking us up. I haven't been out with friends in so long, and I haven't drunk like that for months, so I got a little crazy."

"Seems you're a bad influence on my friends, too. I haven't seen them that messed up in a long time."

There's an awkward silence.

"Um, I need to take a shower. If you want to wait, I'll run you home after," he says.

"Sure, thanks."

I have the best view of the most firm and perfectly shaped ass in boxer briefs after he gets out of bed and strolls out of the room.

Will things be different now? He's friendly this morning, but he's still not giving much away. I pick up the glass of water on the dresser and go to the kitchen. After pouring a fresh glass, I carry it out to the patio. This hangover sucks.

Taking advantage of the view, I try to decide if I should call the agency to get someone else to clean. I haven't been able to bring myself to do it. Every time I think he's a jerk, he does something nice for me. I smell his delicious scent as soon as he comes out the door.

"I'm ready to take you home."

He's in a big hurry to get rid of me. "You're eager to get me out of your house. If I said something mean last night, please forgive me. I'm sure it was the alcohol talking."

There he goes with the stare and silence. I swear I'm starting to think he suffered a brain injury.

"It's just better you go home."

It's just *better*. What the hell does that mean? I want to ask, but I'm sure he'd just stare at me.

"I'd rather walk. I've waited too long to call the agency, so I'll be here Tuesday, but then I won't be back to make you uncomfortable. I'll be sure there are no more rescues, too." I'm pissed, and I'm sure he can tell.

"Skyla, you don't feel well. I don't want you to walk—"

I leave him talking and hurry to the front door. Great, I'm doing the walk of shame in last night's dress. I'm also barefoot, carrying my heels. I should've at least got sex out of it.

What an ass. How many times am I going to let him humiliate me? Furious, I call Eric on my way home.

"Eric, it's Skyla."

"Hey, chick. How are you feeling this morning?"

"Like shit and even more so since I woke up in bed with your jackass friend."

"Dammit, I told him not to touch you!"

I hold the phone away from my ear as Eric yells curse words.

"Eric, we didn't have sex. He slept in the bed with me, but he froze up again this morning. Did I do something last night that would've upset him?"

"I'm trying to figure out what possessed Chase Kalani to sleep in the same bed with you. I doubt he's ever slept in a bed with a girl he hasn't had sex with."

"I think he takes pleasure in rejecting me."

"Sorry, Skyla. I had to call him. I thought Andy was going to be sober to drive you home, but he was just as trashed, so I didn't know what else to do."

I take a deep breath and calm my nerves. He's right. He had to call Chase if he wanted to get me home safely. "I know you had to call him. Thanks for looking out for me, but you didn't answer my question. Did I do something that would've upset him?"

"You called him an asshole as soon as he got to the bar. Then I kept seeing you run your hand through his hair on the way home, but he kept removing it. That's all I witnessed."

"That's all? Are you kidding? I'm going to die. I have to go." I hang up. Nothing nice is going to come out of my mouth. When I get home, I shower and hide under my covers for the rest of the day.

***

I put on my tightest booty shorts and a low cut tank top to clean at Chase's on Tuesday. If he wants to look but not touch, then fine. I'll give him that and hope that it tortures him.

If I'm honest, there's a part of me that hopes it'll cause him to cave and talk to me before he puts his hands all over me. Damn, I miss sex.

Armed with my cleaning supplies and my iPod, I knock on the door. Damn, my palms are sweating. I don't want him to sense my fear or sexual tension. Maybe he won't answer, and I can use the key.

"Hi, Skyla."

Shit. I want to say "Hello, Mr. Moody, Mr. Erratic, and Mr. Pensive. Which one are you today?"

Instead, I scowl. "I'll get to work and get out of your life."

He looks hurt, but I have no clue why. He doesn't follow me or say anything, so I shove my earbuds in and crank up my iPod. I get to work in the downstairs bathroom first.

After finishing there, I walk out and catch a glimpse of something moving. I look to my right and see Chase talking to himself as he paces in his wide open kitchen.

I stand with my hand on my hip and stare at him. I hope he turns around.

Two can play this humiliation game and *bingo*. Check out those big eyes of his looking at me. I smile, and I'm now satisfied, so I go to the living room to clean. I've always been kind to people, but he drives me crazy.

I want to jump his bones because of his hotness, smack him in the face for his rudeness and sooth him over the sadness in his eyes.

I'm one screwed up woman. I crank up rock music and begin dusting. It's such a shame to see all these rooms do nothing but collect dust.

Chase

I hate that she's angry at me, but damn, her feistiness turns me on. I stalk toward the family room. Her back is to me, and all I can focus on is her cute ass shaking back and forth.

She must be enjoying her music, and I'm really enjoying watching her ass move to it. Could those shorts be any tighter? She turns around, and shit, she catches me.

"Are you enjoying the show?" she asks as she yanks out her earbuds.

I start laughing. I can't help it. There are a number of things I could do with that smart mouth of hers and that cute ass. "It's quite entertaining."

"Was it as entertaining as you pacing around the kitchen, talking to yourself?" She throws her free hand to her hip.

I'm going to devour that mouth and fuck her senseless. "I'm sorry I was rude again the other day. It was difficult to wake up with you in my bed." I'm serious now.

She cocks her head to the side. "What does that mean? Never mind because it's not like you'll tell me. I can't keep up with your erratic personality and inept ability at conversation."

She grabs her stuff and walks right past me. The need to be near her is too strong for me to resist, so after a few minutes, I creep my way up the stairs to find her.

I paid a hundred thousand dollars to stalk my housekeeper in my own home. I think it's time for some professional help. Quietly, I walk down the hallway until I hear her.

She's in my damn bedroom!

What the hell is she doing? Did I fail to tell her not to clean in there? The door's cracked, so I look in, and damn she's close to my bed.

I don't believe I'm going anywhere good when I leave this earth, so I'm going to enjoy myself beforehand. I'm kissing her.

The Tide Turns

Skyla

I'll show him. I go into his bedroom on purpose. I hope he finds me in here and is thoroughly uncomfortable with it.

His room is huge, and the furniture is massive. I don't even want to know how many women have been in that king size bed, and I hate that I'm jealous.

I'm about to spray wood cleaner on his dresser when I feel the tap on my shoulder. Practically jumping out of my skin, I turn around. I can't believe I let that happen again, but I didn't expect him to touch me.

His dark, hooded eyes gaze at me intensely as he takes out my earbuds. He steps forward, way into my personal space, and the next thing I know I'm being backed against his bedroom wall.

One hand goes into my hair, and the other squeezes my waist while his lips slam against mine. He forces his tongue into my mouth, pulling me to him in every way.

I drop the wood polish and paper towels that are in my hands and wrap my arms around his neck, my fingers sliding up into his hair.

I kiss him back lustfully, savoring his tongue that's sweeping my mouth. His hair slides right through my fingers like silk. What is it about this man's hair?

His powerful, fit body presses against me, pinning me harder against the wall while his tongue assaults my mouth.

I shove my hips against him and whimper, my body begging for him to put me in his bed. After a couple of minutes, he slows our kiss. Letting go of my lips, he gazes down at me like he's a starving man.

"You're not supposed to clean my room," he says in almost a whisper. I feel his sizzling breath on my skin.

"No one told me, but if this is my punishment, then I'm doing it again."

"Fuck." He groans and grabs my face, putting his hungry mouth on mine once again. I run my hands up under the back of his shirt, my fingertips gliding along his tense muscles.

He halts and releases my lips, allowing me to see the quick rise and fall of his chest as my hands make their descent down his back.

He leans his forehead against mine and brushes the back of his hand down my cheek. "It was difficult to wake up in bed with you, Skyla, because all I wanted to do was touch and taste all of your perfect body. I've been trying for two weeks to resist you."

"Please, don't," I whisper.

"I can't have you, angel."

And just like that he's gone, leaving me all alone in his room. That arrogant ass. I gather my stuff and storm downstairs, finding him on his patio.

"Don't ever speak to me again," I say before I angrily tread back through the house and go out the front door. I need to go back to Cali. The loneliness I feel on this damn island is killing me. A paradise for romance, my ass!

Then Bud leaves me right before we get to be together again. With him being three years older than me, you'd think he wouldn't have given me the time of day, but he dragged me around with him everywhere when we were kids.

Being even a couple of years older than Bud, Lee thought I was a pest, but not my cousin. I cried for a month when he moved here.

He told me I could move to Hawaii, too, in three years, but that's an eternity when you're fifteen and miss someone. Bud was my everything, and I'm so angry at him for dying on me because of his drug addiction.

After slamming my front door, I throw myself onto my couch and cry for all the loss and rejection I've been dealt. My strength is crumbling.

***

A knock at the door wakes me. I don't know how long I've been sleeping. No one visits me, so I'm instantly alarmed. Please don't be the military, please don't be the military. I can't survive another loss. I slowly open the door and see that it's Chase.

Chase

"Hi, can we talk?"

"No." She begins to shut the door on me, so I stick my hand out and catch it.

"Please, I need to apologize."

She looks sad. Her eyes are swollen and red. I hate myself for making her cry.

"Outside," she says before she pushes past me and sits down on her porch steps. I sit next to her.

"Um, I'm sorry. I shouldn't have kissed you like that."

"You're sorry you kissed me?" she asks, looking straight ahead and sounding even angrier.

"No, but it wasn't fair for me to grab you like that. I slept next to you, and I ... I haven't been with a woman in a long time, and you're a very attractive woman, Skyla. I couldn't take it any longer."

I turn toward her to see her expression. She blushes and peers up at me.

"I don't regret you kissing me. What I regret is how you keep giving me the impression you're interested, only to turn right around and push me away."

"I shouldn't be coming on to you because of the shit I'm dealing with, but I selfishly want you around. I came to apologize because I have no business trying to keep you to myself when I know I can't get closer to you."

Her eyes flash back up to mine. "You want to keep me to yourself?" she asks softly.

If she only knew how badly I want to lock her in my room and kiss those juicy lips again.

"Yes, but I need to leave you alone. I came to explain, so you don't think I'm a total jackass. I'm not trying to play some kind of game," I say as I stand up.

She stands, too, and looks pissed. "How can you do this?"

"Do what?"

"How can you feel that way but never plan to see me again?"

"Skyla, I don't need to get to know you better to tell how great you are. I don't deserve someone like you. I'm not a good person."

"I don't see that. You rescued me from those guys on the beach, you doctored my arm and said you'd pay me when I didn't work.

"You fed me lunch. You saved my ass at that bar, and you came here to apologize for kissing me without permission. You're not bad, so why can't you see that?"

She runs her hand up my neck, her fingers sliding into the back of my hair, but it's as if I can feel her touch over my entire body. I feel powerless gazing down at her. Don't give in.

"I have to go, Skyla. You deserve better." I jump into my car and leave. Once again, she's left standing alone. I'm a dirtbag no matter how it plays out.

Skyla

Oh hell no!

I go inside to brush my teeth and straighten myself up. He *will* kiss me again. I walk to his house and pound on the door.

He opens it with a surprised expression on his face, but I still see sadness. I don't look for long before I throw my arms around his neck.

My lips capture his with an unbearable longing. I can't understand my need to be physically and mentally close to this man I barely know, but I'm so drawn to him.

He responds, his tongue quickly circling mine as his strong arms wrap around my waist. My tank top is being pulled tight in the back by his eager hands that grip it.

"Don't push me away. Tell me whatever it is, and I won't judge, but kiss me more first," I say after releasing his lips.

I hear his light chuckle as he shuts the door and grabs my hand, pulling me behind him. He sits on the couch in his family room and looks at the spot next to him, signaling for me to sit down.

I think he's ready to talk, but before he can stop me, I straddle him. I don't know what's come over me.

"I told you to kiss me more first, then talk," I say before I take hold of his face with my hands and kiss him hard, thrusting my tongue into his mouth.

His tongue meets mine as he grabs my hips. I feel his fingers so close to my ass, and I want him to move them down and take hold of it.

I want to know everything about him. A desperate need to hang on to the little bit of him he's giving away controls my every move. Our tangled tongues continue their exploration, every hard stroke a release of aching desire.

I tug on his hair, showing him I'm needy for his touch, hardly able to deter how much I want him. He moans against my mouth and squeezes my hips harder, showing that his restraint is waning, too.

Our lips separate in need of a deep breath, and I slide my hands down the firm planes of his chest while leaning my head down to kiss his neck.

I gently move my wet lips along it until I take hold of his earlobe, carefully pulling it between my teeth before I lick and blow on his ear.

His head falls back as his hands move from my hips to my ass. My wish is granted when he clenches it with his fingers.

Then, I feel it, his erection pushing against me, and all I can think about is being in his bed with him on top of me, sinking into me.

What the hell?

It's been a long time since I've had sex, but there's something more to this. A deeper yearning I've never felt before.

My hands keep moving down his chest, past his stomach until my fingers hit the waistband of his shorts. I softly feather a few kisses back down his neck before he gently takes hold of my wrists.

I sit up and gaze into his pools of darkness that are beginning to show a sign of light, and I can see what I do to him.

"You're unbelievable. That was the hottest thing ever. I mean the hottest," he says before he pulls me forward until my forehead presses against his.

"How am I going to stay away from you?"

"You're not," I whisper.

He shakes his head. Is he saying no? I can sense his struggle, so I sit back up, waiting anxiously for his response.

"I've wanted you since the first moment I saw you. I've wanted you so fucking bad. Will you go on a date with me, Skyla?"

A grin spreads across my face. I'm winning, and Mr. Moody is losing.

Chase

This woman is the sweetest taste of temptation. I walk away from her, leaving her on her porch alone, and she hunts me down. It plays out like a fantasy as she straddles me on my couch. This is one determined chick, and she's got me turned on.

Her mouth is on fire, and god, when she moves it to my neck and ear, I have to put my hands on her ass and squeeze. If I don't, they're going to go everywhere else on her luscious body.

She wants me. She's offering herself to me, so I grab her wrists to stop her from going any further. Any more, and she'll be in my bed. Everything feels right, and I want to do everything to her that I shouldn't.

"Would you go on a date with me, Skyla?"

Where in the hell did that come from? I've never even been on a date. I've had women on my arm for different occasions, but they weren't dates.

She gifts me a beautiful grin that's the best damn present ever. "Yes, but only if you're sure. I probably shouldn't give you time to process this. You might change your mind."

"No, I'm not changing my mind. I want to be near you, Skyla."

"Chase, if you don't want to share your darkest secrets, then don't, but talk to me about everything else. Spend time with me, and kiss me," she says before her lips are back on mine.

I run my hands up into her hair and hold her head, kissing her slowly and softly for several minutes. The kiss in my room was hot, but it was over too quickly.

I've dreamed about having her this way for months, so I relish every second of it. Her warm breath and wet tongue are in sync with mine, made only for my greedy mouth from here on out.

I've never cared an ounce about kissing, but doing it with her is erotic, and I *will* do it again and again. I'm selfish, and when it comes to Skyla, it's a quality I'm not going to be able to change, especially now that I've had a taste.

A Do Over

Skyla

I'm giddy like a teenage girl when Chase drops me off at home. The cheesy grin I kept giving him had to have him laughing inside.

I'm happier than I've been in years, and although I should be guarded from his erratic behavior, I have no desire to be. I want to be close to this man more than I've ever wanted anything.

After losing almost everyone I'm close to, I can't hold back. We don't know how long we have to live and love. I have to take a chance on Chase, even if it means my heart may hurt from it.

He told me to dress nice for our date in Waikiki. He definitely keeps me on my toes. A couple of hours ago, he was barely speaking to me, and now, he wants to take me on a special date.

I put on a flowing, royal blue dress that hits mid-thigh and silver, strappy heels. There hasn't been a reason for me to dress this nice since I got on the island, so I'm excited.

I put loose curls in my long blonde hair and wear silver jewelry. My nerves start getting the best of me right before Chase is to show up, so I call Eric.

"Hi, it's Skyla."

"How's my new friend?"

"I have some news."

"Please tell me you're not moving back to the mainland like you threatened at the bar."

I begin giggling. "No, I need to see how something pans out first."

"What might that be?"

"I had a break through today with your friend. We kissed, and we're going on a date in a few minutes."

"I'm happy for you, Skyla. I knew it was only a matter of time. Chase is used to having what he wants, and I know he wants you. How could he resist a chick as special as you? Don't worry, I'll kick his ass myself if he screws this up."

"You always know the right thing to say. He'll be here any minute, but I'll let you know how it goes."

"No getting smashed tonight," he says, laughing before he hangs up.

I'm grateful that since meeting Eric, he's graciously let me talk to him like he's a chick. I need a girlfriend on this island.

I hear the knock on the door, and my stomach is giving me the feeling that I'm in the ocean. I feel sea sick, so I swallow hard and take a couple of deep breaths before I open it.

Chase

My heart races as I approach Skyla's door. She opens it and smiles. *Wow!* She's stunning. I take in a gasp of air and try to dismiss the dirty thought I'm having of skipping dinner altogether.

"Skyla, you're stunning." My voice cracks, and I realize I said it because I genuinely meant it. It wasn't just the line I've used to get a girl into bed. She's gorgeous and needs to hear it every day.

She takes my hand with a hopeful smile on her face, and the weight of the world settles on me. There's no going back.

Skyla's already given me many chances to be nice, and even though she came after me earlier today, I know in my gut that this is my last chance.

"Nice Corvette. Have you had this hidden in the garage?"

"Yes, I don't drive it every day, especially when I'm picking up a drunk person who might puke in it. It's very new," I say with a chuckle.

"Ha ha, funny. I like it, and I promise I won't get sick in it. That is, as long as you don't feed me too many drinks."

"I don't plan on it. Although, that's when I know how you truly feel." I pull out of her driveway.

"Well, aren't you full of wisecracks? Am I finally seeing Chase's true colors?"

"Maybe." It's been a long time since I've allowed myself to feel or show anything, and it's terrifying me, but I'll hurt her if I don't open up.

Skyla looks out the side window most of the way, which keeps me from getting busted every time I glance over to see her silky thighs showing. I called in a couple of favors last minute for our date.

I've managed to screw up the other times I've fed her, so I'm determined to make this dinner special. We get into Waikiki and drive along the coastline in front of the many resorts.

I pull up for valet parking at the hotel and take her hand to walk inside. The men working eye her, and it annoys me but makes me proud all at the same time.

Even without a lot of money, Skyla looks classy and wholesome, unlike the many women I've screwed around with over the years. For once, I feel lucky to be someone else's date.

We walk to the oceanfront restaurant where I give them my name. They immediately take us past the other tables and down some steps onto the beach. Skyla looks up at me and grins with eager curiosity.

Skyla

Chase picks me up in a black corvette. He also has the red jeep and a silver, Mercedes S550 that I avoided puking in on the way back from the bar.

I've never valet parked before, and I sense it's going to be a day of firsts for me. Lavish floral arrangements grace the lobby, and I can't help but admire their rich colors.

The ornate patterns on the floor are drawing my attention when I hear Chase chuckle. He leans down to my ear.

"I think it's really cute how everything excites you."

"Well, it's lovely in here."

"That's what I mean. You notice and appreciate what many people take for granted.

"The way you spoke of the view from my house, the scenery during the drive here, and even when you described our sandwiches on the beach, you don't miss a thing," he says, squeezing my hand.

As soon as Chase gives his name, the host at the restaurant has us follow him. We walk past the outdoor seating to some steps that lead down to the beach.

We're seated at a candlelit table set with white linen and fancy flatware. It's the only one right on the beach, and it's centered outside of the oceanfront restaurant.

Chase looks like a model straight out of a magazine with his dark hair and eyes that pop from the white dress shirt he's wearing.

I noticed on our walk into the hotel that his khaki pants look as if they were measured and made just for him. They fit him perfectly, and I remember hearing once that designer clothes fit better that way.

I'm sitting across from him, taking in the sight of his chiseled jawline in the candlelight. This man is beyond handsome.

"Why do we get to sit here?" I see all eyes are on us as I look back toward the restaurant, and I imagine they're wondering why Chase and I get the table on the beach.

"Because you're special."

"I'm guessing it's because *you're* special," I say, laughing.

He smirks. "OK, maybe because I'm special it can happen, but I made it happen because you're special."

"Thank you. This is lovely. I've never been anywhere this nice."

"That's a shame." He frowns and reaches his hand across the table to hold mine. "I'm not really special. I made some real estate deals with the owner of this resort, and I managed to reach him after I took you home today. He called in the favor for me."

My guard wants to go up. He's being the complete opposite of how he was when he repeatedly rejected me. I can't figure him out. The waitress comes to take our drink order, and we both get iced tea.

"Do you not drink?" I ask.

He appears uncomfortable and looks away.

"No. I used to drink a lot, but those days are over."

"That's a good thing, right?"

He looks back at me. "Yes, it's a good thing. For me, too much of anything's not good. Well, you might be the exception." He grants me a lascivious look that gives me butterflies and sends chills up my spine.

"That's sweet to say. Um, are your parents alive?"

"No, my mom died of breast cancer about ten years ago, and then my father died from a heart attack three years ago."

I see the grief in his eyes. "I'm sorry. That's extremely odd because my mom died of breast cancer ten years ago, too, and then my father died three years ago in Afghanistan.

"He was a contracted employee for the government. He worked construction, and on his way to a job site, the vehicle he was in hit an IED. I was told he died instantly. My brother joined the Army then, and that's basically how I ended up here."

He squeezes my hand. "I'm sorry, Skyla. You're even younger than me, and it's unfair you had to lose your family at such a young age."

The tears moisten my eyes. His words are so sincere, and I know he understands exactly what I've been through. A few drops fall to my cheek, and I quickly wipe them away.

"I'm sorry. I haven't had anyone to talk to about my parents in a long time, and knowing you can relate makes me sad for you, too. My brother won't discuss my parents with me," I say.

He leans over and wipes away another tear with the pad of his thumb. His touch is soothing, and all I want to do is curl up in his arms. I feel I've made him terribly sad.

"Are you OK? I'm sorry I asked about your parents. I don't want our date to be depressing."

"I'm fine, Skyla. I hate that we're in the same club, but it's comforting to know that if I needed to talk about losing them, you'd understand."

"You keep saying sweet things, and it's a little jarring after the way you've been since I've met you."

"I know, and I'm sorry. I still feel you deserve someone with less baggage, but I can't resist being close to you. It's selfish of me, but that's one behavior I'm still working on improving."

"Everyone has shit from their past. I mean, look what grief we carry from our parents' death. I'm no better than you. Other than knowing I'm going to college, I'm a lost twenty year old."

The waitress arrives with our entrées. Feeling as if our date is turning a little too serious, I'm relieved to see her at our table.

She sits down our platter of seafood for two, and I have no idea what I'm looking at. I try to hold in my giggle until the waitress leaves, and as soon as she walks away, it erupts from my mouth.

Chase is grinning at me. "What's so funny?"

"I have no idea what any of this food is other than I recognize the shrimp. Sorry, I'm not a very worldly person."

"I'll tell you what you're eating." He proceeds to point to each item as he speaks. "This is lobster, and this is onaga, which is long-tail red snapper. It's all steamed with kaffir lime leaves.

"The kaffir lime is a fruit native to some Southeast Asian countries. These are different aioli sauces. They're kind of like different types of mayonnaise."

"OK. It looks delicious. I want to know all about the Hawaiian culture, so tell me more about the foods."

Chase educates me throughout dinner, and I try to absorb all the information. He's even smarter than I thought, and I find myself smiling often over how he's opening up to me.

The waitress comes back with dessert, and my hand goes straight across my stomach.

"I'm so full, but whatever this is, it looks delicious."

"It's coconut cake filled with coconut-amaretto cream."

"I love anything coconut, and I also love amaretto flavor, so I'm certain this will be like sex for me."

Chase raises his eyebrows and smirks.

"Well, if this is what gets you going, then I'm in trouble. I don't know if I can compete with this cake."

"Maybe I'll get a chance to compare," I say with an alluring smile.

His smirk instantly disappears. "You're sexy, Skyla."

"So are you, Chase." From the light of the candle, golden speckles in his lust filled eyes glimmer. We stare at each other in silence while I take bites of my cake, and I'm ready for dinner to be over. I want physical contact with him.

"Would you like to walk the beach here, or would you prefer the beach by my place?"

"I would definitely like to walk the beach here at some point, but I work tomorrow, so maybe it'd be better if we head back."

"I have some work to do tomorrow, too, so that sounds good. Are you finished with your 'better than sex' cake?" he asks with a devilish grin.

"It satisfied some of my craving, anyway."

He gives me another desire filled stare and takes my hand for the walk to the car. His touch sparks a tingling sensation to course through me, settling heavy between my thighs, and I can't help but imagine him remedying the situation.

Chase

We start the drive home, and the only thing I can think about is making her feel better than that damn cake tastes.

I'll make her forget all about the fucking cake. There's no denying the sexual tension between us, and it's suffocating me at the moment.

I need a release, and it needs to be with Skyla underneath me in my bed. I glance to her, and she seems in deep thought. I have to get my mind off of sex.

"I had to give Eric and Andy hell for getting you drunk when you're underage. It wasn't safe, either."

She giggles. "I think it was the other way around."

"They took you too far away and let you drink way too much."

"I guess I'm extremely lucky then that no one kidnapped me from the bar and sold me off as a sex slave."

Her comment leaves me chuckling.

"Where did you come up with that idea?"

"I've heard it happens to girls my age who are in strange cities. I saw it in a movie. I had you walk me home that first night instead of driving me because I was worried you might sell me off."

I glance over at her and realize she's serious.

"I don't need the money."

Her head snaps toward me. "You're being facetious. I know you wouldn't do something that awful."

"You're right. I'm bad but not that bad. You've mentioned sex a couple of times tonight. Is there something you're trying to tell me?"

"Let me just say it's been a long time for me, too. I can't understand why that's the case with you. I imagine you could have almost any woman you want on this island."

"Time will tell. I've never wanted a relationship, and I gave up sleeping around many months ago. You're a lot like Eric. You tell it like you see it even when others don't ask to hear it."

I glance over, and she looks in deep thought again.

"Are you never planning on being in a relationship?" she asks.

"I haven't felt like I deserve a relationship."

"I've had a few boyfriends. They were assholes."

"What about friends? Do you have a lot of them in California?" I ask.

"I have one close girlfriend named Brooke and a few that I'm not as close to. I've always gotten along better with guys. I grew up with mostly males, so I'm more comfortable around them."

"That's cool. I'm an only child, but I've been fortunate to have great friends."

"I wish Brooke could live here. I could fix her up with Eric."

That's one worry I can scratch off the list. I guess she doesn't have any romantic feelings for Eric after all. She seems upset since I told her I've never wanted a relationship.

I feel an urgency to clarify that, so I pull over on the side of the road, my heart pounding in my chest. She immediately looks at me.

"Why are we stopping?"

"You seemed upset after I said I've never wanted a relationship. I should've been clearer in expressing that I felt that way in the past, not now."

"OK," she says while picking at the hem of her dress.

I've made her nervous. "I like you a lot, Skyla. I'd like to see where this can go."

"I like you, too. I've tried to show you," she says softly.

"You have, and I feel like a jackass for pushing you away, so I wanted to explain what I meant about a relationship. I don't want to punish myself anymore and miss out on a chance with you."

"You give the impression you were an assassin or something. If you'll let me, I'll be here whenever you're ready to tell me what's made you think so badly of yourself. Then I'll be here to tell you that you're a great person."

I cup the side of her face. "You're amazing, Skyla, so damn amazing." Even in the dim light of the car, her blue eyes shine up at me.

She leans over and parts her lips, urging me in. Our kiss ignites quickly, our mouths crashing against each other's as the sexual tension swells between us.

I've always been rough with women. They did what I wanted, when I wanted and where I wanted. I could've ravished Skyla and tossed her aside in a flash, but her kindness and honesty make me want to do better.

We kiss for several minutes, and when I let her go, we're both breathing hard. She's too sweet for me.

"Dammit, Skyla, I fuck; I don't date."

"I disagree. Tonight's been a great date. You could've fucked me when I was drunk, but you chose not to.

"You grabbed my wrists earlier today, and I was definitely reaching for something ... something *hard*." She tries to be serious but starts giggling.

"Shit, Skyla, you have a dirty mouth. Now that I've allowed myself to be close to you, I want all of you."

"That turns me on," she says.

An arousing look comes my way, and I swear I'm ready to spank her ass. I'm trying to behave.

"I'm getting the impression that you're not as innocent as I thought, so I promise I'll have you soon."

"Swear?"

I believe this is my payback for what I've been doing to her the last couple of weeks. I shake my head and smirk as I pull back onto the road.

I'd like to tell her to quit being a tease, but I have a feeling she's more than willing to mess around. There's no way it compares to how badly I want her.

"I should go on to my house since it's getting late. Can I take a rain check for the walk on the beach?" she asks.

"Of course. Did I say something to upset you?"

"Not at all. It's just ... after that kiss, it'd be dangerous for me to be near your home. I don't think I'd want to leave, and we both work tomorrow."

"That's probably a good idea. I wouldn't want you to leave, either. I want to take my time when I get the opportunity to pleasure you."

I bring her hand up to my mouth and kiss it. I glance over, and even in the dim light, I see she's blushing.

We're both quiet the rest of the way. I pull into her driveway and look at her for several seconds. I want to take her home and tuck her into my bed.

"I'll be home all evening tomorrow, or any other day this week if you feel like going on that walk," I say.

She shows me that cute smile again and kisses my cheek. For the first time that I can remember, I'm looking forward to what tomorrow brings.

Confessions

Skyla

I wake up the next morning thinking of Chase. Since February, my first thought has been of Bud. I realize I'm starting to heal, but I'm still fragile, so I hope I can trust Chase not to break my heart.

It took me hours to fall asleep last night from the happiness and sexual frustration I felt. I should probably be ashamed for wanting to go to bed with him this soon but I'm not.

I can't seem to get close enough to that man, and what woman wouldn't want a night with him? He couldn't be any more desirable.

I get out of the shower and see I have a text. I seldom get them since I have very few people in my life. My heart flutters when I see it's Chase's number.

Chase: *I had a great time with you last night, and you were my first thought this morning. I hope you have a good day. Keep that iPod turned down. I don't want you falling into anyone else's bathtub. You're only allowed in mine and under different circumstances.*

I grin from ear to ear. I'm going to fall for him fast. Please, please don't crush my heart into a million pieces.

Me: *I had a hard time falling asleep last night from that amazing date. You were my first thought, and I don't think I can stay away today, so if you're still up for that walk this evening, then I'm game. I'll try not to injure myself beforehand. You have a good day, too.*

Chase: *I'll be waiting.*

***

The day drags, and he's all I can think about. I go home to shower again, and Eric calls.

"So, how was it?"

"Eric, it was unreal, and I'm in deep. He was different last night. He was sweet and really talked to me. We have a lot in common, too."

"That's great, Skyla. You have no idea what it means to me to know we might see a happy Chase."

"I'm dying to know what has made him feel so awful about himself, but I know he needs to tell me, and I think he will when he's ready."

"It might take a while, so please be patient with him."

"Listen, I think I'm ready to get back on my board. Can we surf together Saturday?"

"Hell yeah, chick. I need to see your skills."

"I might be a little rusty at first. It's been nine months."

Eric is quiet. "Are you still there?" I ask.

"Um, yeah. I was thinking about something. I'll see you Saturday."

It's five o'clock when I finish getting ready. I put on my red spaghetti strap sundress and flip flops before I message Chase.

Me: *Hi, still up for that walk? I'll bring tacos.*

Chase: *Yes, and tacos sound great. Do you want me to pick you up?*

Me: *No, I'm a big girl, remember?*

Chase: *You keep reminding me. See you soon.*

I get the tacos and drive to his house as quickly as I can. He's smiling at me when he opens the door, his perfect white teeth shining against his dark skin.

He smells enticing, and his athletic shorts and tight t-shirt are hugging all the firm, muscular parts of his fit body just right.

"Hi, Skyla, come in."

"Hi." I follow him to the kitchen and set the food down. I'm caught off guard when he pulls me into his arms and hugs me. I could stay here forever.

After a long embrace, he leans back and gazes down at me. "I've wanted to hug you since we talked about our parents. I hope you don't mind."

I know I'll give this man whatever he wants if he keeps saying sweet things like that.

"No, I don't mind. You can kiss me, too, if you'd like."

He smiles at me before his lips are on mine. They're soft, wet and wonderful. Our kiss intensifies, tongues swirling together as he pulls me in closer to him.

My fingers go straight into his hair, gliding through the silken strands before I scrunch it back up into my hands, tugging it, bringing his face as close to mine as possible.

His tongue darts in and out of my mouth as his hands travel down over my ass. He lets me go and looks down at me with that same starving look he had when he kissed me in his bedroom.

"We should eat."

I try to slow down my breathing before I speak.

"We should." It's all I can say. Every part of my body is screaming for him to touch it. I know he sees it in my eyes when he takes my face into his hands and kisses me again, this time even harder.

I run my hands up under the back of his t-shirt, and unlike when we were in the bedroom, he doesn't stop me. Turning my body, he pushes me up against the island in the middle of his kitchen and settles his leg between mine.

I feel his erection pressing against me as he runs his hands down my neck to my breasts and massages them while kissing on my ear.

My head falls back, his touch stirring up a hot sensation throughout my yearning body, eliciting a whimper.

"Your whimpering drives me crazy, Skyla."
Chase quickly releases me when we hear a noise behind us.

"Shit, sorry dude. I didn't know you had company."

I recognize Eric's voice immediately. He'd come in the back door off of the kitchen, which leads out to the patio. Glancing up at Chase, I see he's glaring at him.

"Hi, Eric. How are you?" I ask without turning around and while trying not to giggle.

"Hi, Skyla. I'm not as good as you two," he replies, chuckling. "I'll come back tomorrow, bro, and I'll knock first."

"That's a good idea," Chase says.

I look up again and see that he's now smirking at Eric. I'm glad he's seeing the humor in this. I hear the door shut. Slowly, I look up at Chase and giggle with embarrassment.

"We should eat," he says before he leans over and kisses the top of my head.

Damn you, Eric. Feeling the pulsing ache between my legs only makes me want Chase more.

"OK." I lightly sigh with disappointment. He tells me to sit while he heats up our food. Taking deep breaths, I try to calm my nerves, but the ache between my legs is not fading.

We sit across from each other, and he's quiet. I don't like it, and I'm paranoid he'll shut me out again. I know he wants me, but he seems to be fighting a battle. I don't like the enemy one bit, and I'm determined to help him conquer it.

"How was your day?" I ask.

"It was good since I had you to think about and a pretty image in my head." He gives me a faint smile.

"Every time you say sweet things to me, it makes me want you more," I say with longing.

Chase stops moving and stares at me for a few seconds before he speaks. "You are so damn sexy, Skyla. I'm trying not to take you to my bed, but if you don't stop, I'm carrying you there, and we won't be sleeping this time."

My eyes widen. He's the sexy one.

"Who said I don't want that?" My gaze is locked firmly with his.

"Fuck. Are you finished eating? I think we need to go for that walk. I need to talk to you about something."

"I'm finished." I'm also nervous. Is he getting ready to reveal his big secret? He takes my hand and shakes his head.

"I'm beginning to think our paths crossed so you can torture me every day with temptation."

"You're torturing yourself, mister."

"Not for long, angel ... not for long."

Chase

I take Skyla's hand and lead her to the beach. Feeling her skin lights me up, but I'm trying to stay focused on the fact that she has a right to know the way I used to live. I'm hoping she'll still want to be with me after, so I can fuck her very soon.

The waiting is torture, especially when she's taunting me. I feel as if Skyla's my new drug, and I don't know if I can handle that constant urge. Wanting to see her and touch her every day is about to drive me insane.

She has a right to know about Bud, too, but there's no way I can talk about him any time soon. I haven't had to tell that story since I went into rehab right after he died.

"Um, Skyla, I feel like I should tell you some things about my past."

She looks up at me and pulls a stray hair away from her face. Her expression shows curiosity but also concern. "OK."

"I used to do a lot of bad things ... unhealthy things that hurt not only me but others around me."

I feel her squeeze my hand tighter.

"Like what?"

"I was only fifteen when my mom died, and I took it really hard, so I started drinking. By the time I was twenty, I was out of control with it, and it was hard to hide, so I started experimenting with drugs, thinking I could conceal that better.

"First, it was pot. When my dad died a couple of years later, I needed something more to numb the pain. I also needed it to keep me going, so I could work.

"The alcohol and pot only made me depressed and lazy. A friend introduced me to cocaine, and it seemed like the perfect fix.

"A drawback to being wealthy is that you can get drugs whenever you want them and not the cheap stuff, either. I was using heavily, but I went to rehab, and I've been clean close to a year now.

"I'm fortunate in that my brain doesn't seem to be wired for addiction the way it is for a lot of people. It was easier for me to stop than I expected.

"I'll never let myself be that person again." I wait for her to respond. I filled her head with enough garbage to process.

"Chase, I hate to think of how hard life's been for you since your parents died. I'm sorry you had to go through that all those years. To think you suffered and didn't really live makes me sad for you."

"You feel bad for me?"

"Yes. You've been through a lot. It's great you got clean, and I don't know why you think you're a bad person. You made poor choices, but it started when you were young because of a tragedy, and it spiraled from there. You need to cut yourself some slack. Your strength is amazing."

"I'm not scaring you off?"

"No. Did you think I wouldn't want anything to do with you because of that?" She seems genuinely surprised.

"Not entirely. In the beginning I thought so, but you've made me feel like I could tell you, so I was hoping you wouldn't run away."

"I have even more respect for you, Chase. At a young age, you lost the people you love and depend on the most. You went to a dark place to take away the pain, but you found the strength to crawl your way out of the hole. That's commendable."

"I can't tell you what it means to me that you're not upset, but there's something else I need to tell you that goes with it. Because of doing the drugs, I also slept with a lot of women.

"I feel horrible about it now, but I can't change the past. I want you to know that I always used protection, and I'm clean."

"It's fine, Chase. No offense, but I assumed you've slept with a lot of women. You're too good-looking not to have women throwing themselves at you, especially those who are also greedy."

Skyla stops walking and wraps her arms around me, hugging me tight. I can't even comprehend how I can tell her all of that, and instead of her being angry and leaving me, she tells me how sorry she is for what I went through. I don't know how she can have more respect for me.

She'd probably feel differently if I told her the whole truth. Would she want to be near me if I told her that I supplied the drugs that killed my friend?

I'm too selfish to find out right now. I can't risk losing her. I hug her back and stroke her long hair, feeling so much relief that she's at least sticking around.

She pulls away and gazes up at me.

"I'm relieved you're not in some kind of mob or sex slave business."

I grab her face and give her one deep kiss. She giggles against my mouth, and I swear that sound is fucking adorable. "Skyla, you're an angel. A very, very cute one."

Explorations

Skyla

That wasn't so bad. I don't know what I expected to hear, but he led me to believe it'd be worse. He really is brave. He doesn't know it, but I believe it's already too late for me to ever walk away from him.

After we go back in from finishing our walk, Chase seems uncomfortable. I imagine he's not sure if he should touch me again. He has to be aware that it'd be hard for us to stop.

I decide I should go to make things easier on the both of us. After all he told me, it doesn't feel like the right night to end up in his bed. I don't want him to remember anything negative from the day we make love.

"I think I should go since I have to work again tomorrow, but then I'm off for four days in a row."

He smiles at me. "I have to go into Waikiki tomorrow evening for a business dinner, but if you'll spend some time with me those other days, I'd be a happy man."

"You know what a busy social life I lead, but I'll try to fit you in," I say, kidding as we walk to the front door.

"I wouldn't want to interfere with Eric and Andy's lunch delivery on Saturday."

"I might share with you, too, if you're nice and rub sunscreen on me again." I wrap my arms around his waist and peer up at him.

He smiles. "That's asking for a lot. You have no idea how hard that was on me."

His hands run up into the back of my hair, his expression turning serious, before he brushes a few kisses on my lips.

"My hands covered in lotion, gliding along your smooth skin that felt like silk," he says barely above a whisper, his hot breath warming my skin once again.

My body starts trembling. His words dance along every one of my nerves, awakening them to beckon for his touch. "Chase," I whisper.

He bends down a little, grazing his lips up my neck until they hover above my ear. "Then you were right between my legs. Pure. Fucking. Torture."

One of his hands drop, and the next thing I feel is his fingertips on my thigh, trailing up under my sun dress, his mouth still lingering on my neck.

The pulsing ache is back with a vengeance. His fingers move slowly along my inner thigh until they brush my panties and trail down my other thigh.

"Chase," I whisper again. I don't know why I'm saying his name. Do I want him to stop or keep going?

My body jerks when I feel his hand cupping my wet panties, his thumb rubbing circles on the outside of them. His mouth is back on my ear.

"You're really wet, angel. I think I should play nice and finish what I've started."

His words draw a chill across my skin, and I feel my legs trying to go, my body still trembling. He moves his free hand to the nape of my neck and holds me while his other hand taunts me through the wet silk of my panties.

His fingers slowly slide inside of them and sink into me. I whimper before sucking in a gasp of air.

"Fuck, Skyla, you're so warm inside and tight around my fingers." He begins moving them in and out of my scorching flesh, crippling my control. I'm helpless and dependent on his touch. I think I'd die if he stopped now.

My eyes are clenched shut, and my breathing's labored as the pleasure builds and emanates, spreading like a wildfire. His thumb is circling my clit all while his fingers plunge into me repeatedly.

"Open your eyes, Skyla. I'm going to see your face and those baby blues when you come for me."

I slowly open them, feeling bashful. He's staring at me with desire in his eyes. This is as much for him as it is for me.

My lids are heavy as the pleasure seizes me, tipping me over the cusp, but I never look away from his hungry gaze.

"That's it. Come for me, Skyla. I've never seen anything as fucking beautiful as your face is right now."

Waves of stinging pleasure wash over me again and again, my body writhing against his commanding fingers. I realize he's holding me up as I come down from my high, collapsing against his chest.

His fingers slide out of me, and I feel his hands under the back of my dress, clenching my ass. I'm sated and warm against his chest, wanting nothing more than to curl up with him in his bed.

I feel his erection against me and realize how difficult this has to be for him. I'm not sure if I should return the favor.

He pulls back from me and leans down to capture my lips, his hands still on my ass, pushing it against his hard-on. He kisses me slowly and skillfully for a couple of minutes.

"I know this can't be easy for you. Do you want me to make you feel better?" I ask.

"Not tonight. You have no idea what you've already done for me. I'll have that image in my head forever. I didn't mean for that to happen. I couldn't resist and wanted you to feel good."

I smile up at him sheepishly. I've never experienced anything that sensual and intimate. I've had sex before, but those times don't compare to this moment between us.

"Thank you. That felt incredible, and I'll make it up to you soon. I—I better go." Leaning up, I plant a gentle kiss on his lips. "Thank you for a great evening."

"Thank you for being so understanding about my past. I care what you think about me, Skyla."

"I think you're great, Chase. Goodnight." I walk out the door, very thankful that I drove tonight. All my energy has been zapped, and my legs feel like Jell-O.

Chase

Throughout the night, I'm tormented from pleasure and pain as I continually see Skyla's face when she came from my touch.

If a woman didn't get off while I was fucking her, then she was out of luck, but with Skyla, I could touch her all day long knowing I'm making her feel that damn good. This strong desire to take care of her and please her has taken over.

I wake up exhausted, and I'm disappointed I won't see her. I want to do something nice for her since she didn't run away after hearing about my past.

Aware of her love for the ocean, and knowing she's going to school for marine biology, I get an idea. After making a call to arrange things, I text Skyla to call me when she can. Soon after, my phone rings.

"Hello, angel."

"Hi."

"Do you have plans tomorrow?"

"No, I was hoping to see you," she replies.

"How early would you be willing to see me?"

I hear that cute giggle I love so much.

"I guess it depends if you make it worth my while."

"You're driving me crazy. Do you know that? I think it's worth getting up early for this." Now, I picture her lying underneath me in my bed, and I'm blaming her this time.

"OK, I trust you."

"I'll pick you up at 5:30 in the morning. Wear a bathing suit and something warm over it."

"Wow, that's early, so this better be good."

"I'll make a deal with you. If you don't enjoy yourself during our outing, then I'll make sure you do when we get back."

She's silent for a few seconds. "Um, it's a deal. I'll see you in the morning, Chase."

Skyla

As I wait for Chase to pick me up, I yawn several times. This is too early to be out of bed, but I have a strong feeling it'll be worth it.

I have on denim shorts and a grey sweatshirt over my hot pink bikini, and my hair is braided in a side fishtail.

I see him pull into the driveway, and I swear my heart skips a beat. Just thinking about him gets me breathless.

He's smiling when I get into the car, and it still takes me by surprise since he seldom smiled the first couple of weeks I knew him.

"Good morning," he says.

"Good morning, Chase." I give him a peck on the cheek after I buckle up.

"I was sure you'd be angry at me for getting you up this early, so it's nice to see that smile on your face. Have any idea what we might be doing?"

"Um, I had one idea. I imagine you have a boat, so I wonder if we're going out on it, but something tells me it isn't that obvious."

"We are going out on a boat, but it's not mine. I do have my own, and I hope I get a chance to take you out on it."

"I can't wait to see what we're doing." I feel butterflies in my stomach as we pull up near the docks and park. The only light I see are from a couple of boats that people are moving around on and the dock lights.

We walk to one of the boats, and Chase tells me to wait while he goes to speak to someone. He has a discussion with an older gentleman and waves me over.

"Ron, this is Skyla. She has no idea what we're doing here, so let me have a minute to make sure I'm not going to have to take her back home."

"No problem," Ron says with a chuckle.

"Nice to meet you," I say before he walks away. Oh no. This doesn't sound good. "Chase, what are we doing?" I'm sure he sees the anxiety wash over me.

"How do you feel about sharks?"

"Um, I don't want to be eaten by one, but otherwise, I think they're fascinating. Why?"

"If you're OK with it, we're going to get into the cage that's on the side of that boat and go under water to swim with the sharks. If you're not comfortable with it, we don't have to.

"I swear it won't upset me. I know I'm springing this on you, but I thought with what you're studying at college, you'd enjoy it."

"That sounds awesome. I'd love to."

He grins and pulls me into a hug, obviously pleased with my decision. I love the feel of his strong biceps wrapped around me.

"I had a feeling you'd like the idea."

I see several men hard at work as they move around the boat. Chase helps me up the steps.

"Welcome aboard. I'm glad you decided to give it a try. He said you're a risk taker," Ron says, laughing.

"He did, huh?" I glance to Chase. We sit down before he smiles and squeezes my leg.

"It's true. You like to risk your safety," he says with a shrug of his shoulders.

"You worry about me an awful lot."

"I don't want anything to happen to you, but I feel this is a safe thing to do, unlike you walking alone in the dark on the beach." He leans over and kisses my cheek. I don't think he could be any cuter.

Ron walks back over to us. "We'll be riding out about three miles before we begin this morning, so I'm going to go over all the safety precautions as we take off. Since it's just the two of you, there isn't any sense in me doing it over the intercom."

After Ron finishes giving us instructions, I pull my hands up into the sleeves of my sweatshirt, preparing myself for the chilly ride.

Chase notices and picks up my legs, swiveling them up onto his lap. He wraps one arm around them while his other arm pulls me tight against him.

I haven't had a male look after me in a long time. It's comforting, so I lay my head against his shoulder and soak in his kindness and warm embrace as the salty, cool mist showers us.

Some time passes before Ron walks past us.

"We'll be stopping in a minute. You must be a special woman to get this boat to yourself."

I glance to Chase. "What did he mean by that? Is there normally a lot of people on these tours?"

"Yes, but you don't need to worry about that."

"Chase, did you reserve this whole boat for us?"

"Yes. I didn't think I'd be able to last minute, but there wasn't as many signed up for this one, so they managed to move people to the later times."

"That means you had to pay for everyone. How many are normally on here?"

"Um, twenty or so. Don't worry about how many, and I really wish I'd told him not to mention that." He seems a bit aggravated at Ron now.

"You had to have paid at least a couple of grand for us to do this. Why? I would've been content on here with other people."

"I know, but you wouldn't get as much time with the sharks as I think you deserve." He smiles as he tucks hair behind my ear. "Also, the selfish me wants to be alone with you."

"Thank you, but I don't need you to do things like this. It's very sweet, but you can't spend that kind of money on me. It isn't right." I look away from him. I'm embarrassed.

"I have it to spend, and I wanted to do something nice for you since you were understanding about my past. Actually, I'll want to keep doing nice things for you because you're so special."

"I'm flattered and grateful, but you need to know that I'm probably the least high maintenance woman you're going to meet.

"My family wasn't wealthy, so I don't have high expectations when it comes to having expensive things or doing expensive activities. I'm fairly easy to please."

"All the more reason I want to do it, and all the more reason you deserve it. Please enjoy yourself and not think about that, OK?"

His smile is gone. He was so excited earlier, and now I've hurt his feelings. Although this is all too much, it was sweet of him. I take his chin and turn his face toward me.

"Thank you. I'm just overwhelmed that you did something so thoughtful. No one has ever treated me this way. You're very sweet, Chase."

Leaning over, I bury my face against his neck, kissing it a few times. He squeezes my thigh a little harder.

"As good as that feels, Skyla, you need to stop. If you don't, I'm having them turn the boat around. There are things I want to do to you, and I can't do them here."

He has me aroused now, and I'm certain of what he has in mind, but I want to hear him say it, so I whisper in his ear.

"What exactly do you want to do to me, Chase?"

He turns and locks his gaze with mine. After a few seconds, he leans over and whispers back to me as he cups my face with his hand.

"I find myself wanting to make love to you, which is a first for me. I want to do it gently and slowly, savoring every second of it, but after that ... I plan to fuck you hard."

My heart begins racing. I feel my lip quivering, and the aching pulse returns between my thighs. I swallow hard before I conjure up the nerve to look into his eyes.

"I don't think I'm going to enjoy myself this morning."

He lets go of my face and looks at me with a worried expression.

"You told me if I don't enjoy myself on this outing, then you'll make sure I do when we get back. I have this unbearable ache between my legs that needs relief, so I need not to enjoy this."

He gives me a boyish grin. "It's difficult for me, but I guess I could let you have both."

Playfully, I push him away. "I'm so sure it'd be difficult for you." I roll my eyes. I have to do something to break some of this sexual tension, or I'm really not going to enjoy myself because sex is all I'm going to be able to think about, especially after what he did to me the other night.

"OK, back to the task at hand … what kind of sharks are we going to see?"

"They are mostly Galapagos and maybe sandbar."

When we stop, we get on our snorkel gear. Ron tells us that the water is around 650 feet deep where we're at. I bravely step up and say that I want to be the first to climb down the ladder into the cage.

Once Chase is in, we immediately see the sharks coming up below us. Some of them look to be as long as eight feet, and they circle around us, sometimes gliding right along the bars of the cage.

I'm in awe over this experience. Blessed isn't a strong enough word for how I feel to be a guest in this magical ocean with these marvelous creatures.

Chase comes up to me several times and wraps his arms around my waist. We smile and point like two kids at the zoo for the first time. I feel as if Bud's with me when I'm in or near the ocean.

He became a part of it, and I know there's no other way he would've wanted to die. I just wish it didn't have to be so soon. He lit up the world, and the more Chase opens up to me, the more he reminds me of Daniel.

Since we were the only ones on the boat, we get in a few different times, taking small breaks in between. I'm cold after we get out for good, so I put on my sweatshirt and curl up against Chase again.

He feels warm and safe, and for the first time in a long time, I feel full. The emptiness in my heart is gone.

We get into the Mercedes, and I'm giving him what I'm sure is that big, goofy grin of mine. I lean over and kiss his cheek. "Thank you. That was unbelievable. I had a really great time."

"You're welcome. I had a great time, too."

"To be that far out in the ocean and that close to the sharks gave me a little time to be a part of something so much larger than myself.

"I can't believe I'm telling you this, but I've wanted to be a mermaid since I was a little girl. I'd be one very happy mermaid."

Chase chuckles.

"I know it's silly."

"No it's not. I was thinking of how damn sexy you'd be as a mermaid. It's a sight I'd like to see. Of course, only if I can stay in the ocean with you."

I feel a tug at my heart. Bud called me Nixie. The legend is that Nixie's a water dwelling spirit that appears in human form.

When I was eight years old, Bud and I looked up mermaids on the internet. As soon as he stumbled upon the name, he started calling me that. Bud gave nicknames to everyone he knew.

"Hey, sexy mermaid, you OK over there?"

I snap out of my trance and glance to Chase.

"Yes, sorry."

"If you don't feel comfortable doing this, then tell me, but would you want to grab some things and get cleaned up at my house?

"As you know, I have awesome bathrooms. You can shower or soak in the Jacuzzi tub. I'm not ready to give you up."

"I'd like that. I should get to enjoy them since I'm the one who cleans them," I say jokingly.

I grab some things from my house, and we drive to Chase's. My nerves are starting to get the best of me. I have no doubt we'll be fooling around today, but how soon, and how far we go is the significant question.

More than a Mere Taste

Chase

I've had the best morning with Skyla. She's the tranquil light at the end of the tunnel. She takes nothing for granted. I still don't deserve her, but I vow to be better because of her.

As soon as we enter the house, she looks at me as if she doesn't know what to do next. I take hold of one of her hands. "When I'm finished showering, I'll run out and get us some breakfast. Does that sound good?"

"Sure. I'm hungry since I got up so early."

"Go take whichever bathroom you want, except for mine, or you'll have company."

She gives me a nervous smile before we both walk upstairs to the bedrooms. After pleasuring her the other night and our conversation about sex this morning, there will be no way for me to keep my hands off of her. I'm selfish, so I'm sure I'll take more than a mere taste this time.

After I finish showering, I leave to get breakfast. Skyla's sitting on the patio when I return. I get a strange, warm feeling seeing her so comfortable at my home. She belongs here with me.

"I have breakfast. We can eat out here if you want." Damn she smells enticing, and she's wearing some revealing ass clothing, too. She has on a low cut, light blue top that gives me a great boob shot as I stand over her. Then she has more of those damn tiny denim shorts on.

"Thank you. I'm starving. I guess it's from all that flailing around I did in the shark cage."

"Between the two of us, there was a lot of that going on," I say, chuckling.

After we eat, we stare at the ocean in silence. I'm in amazement over how much Skyla loves the ocean the way I do. I'm hopeful that one of these days, we'll surf together. She's by far the coolest woman I've ever met.

I look over and find that she's sound asleep. I quietly laugh. I guess I got her up too early, and then I imagine the sound of the waves put her to sleep, or maybe it was the flailing.

I have to laugh again. I can't recall ever feeling this happy. I want to lie next to her, so I pick her up, and she slightly opens her eyes.

"You can go back to sleep, baby. I'm going to put you in bed."

Yawning, she wraps her arms around my neck and closes her eyes again. I can't get over how much she trusts me, and it honestly annoys me a little.

She's going to end up hurt by trusting the wrong person. Her kindness makes her naïve. She believes her goodness is in everyone, and it's unfortunately not true.

I gently place her in my bed and watch her roll over away from me. After climbing in, I wrap my arm around her, pulling her close. I can't resist nuzzling my nose into her neck and hair. Damn, she feels and smells unbelievable.

It surprises me when she starts to roll back over. I let her go and back up. She stares at me, inches from my face before she leans right in and kisses me.

I wasn't going to mess around with her right now, but she wants to, and I'm not about to turn her down. My hand runs up into her hair as I pull her head close, deepening our kiss.

Her hand goes under the back of my shirt, and just like the other times, her touch sets me on fire. I have a constant burn for Skyla. I'm not numb or high, so I feel her touch awakening every nerve on my body.

Letting her mouth go, I slowly graze my lips along her jaw until I'm near her ear. "You make me feel alive, Skyla," I whisper before my lips move to her neck. She rolls onto her back, inviting me in to touch and taste all of her.

Sitting up on my knees, I pull my shirt off before I reach down and pull hers up over her head. Shit, she has a hot, lacy bra on. She reaches behind her and unhooks it, throwing it off my bed. The deepest breath escapes me as I admire her.

A smile appears on her face. "I've been waiting to get up close and personal with your chest and abs, and they're about to be on top of me. Your body is sensational," she says, gazing up at me.

"Really? You want to talk about my body while you're topless in my bed with the most gorgeous set of tits?"

In a second, my eager mouth is on one, and my hand is on the other. Her nipple hardens against my swirling tongue, and her fingers pull on my hair.

"Fuck," I groan. "Skyla, my body wants to explode, but I want to go slow and enjoy the feel and taste of your skin."

"Do whatever you want to me. I just want you, Chase … more than anything."

"Shit, don't tell me to do whatever I want." My mouth takes in all of her magnificent breast as my lust rushes to the surface.

I swear I'm going to bury myself inside of her. She tilts her head back against the pillow, arching against my mouth while tugging even harder on my hair.

"Do you have a condom?" she asks as she gasps for air.

"Yes."

"Don't take your time, Chase. Just fuck me hard."

"Damn, Skyla, you are the hottest woman." I'm off the bed, pulling off the rest of my clothes. She's wiggling out of her shorts and lacy underwear just as fast. Clothes off, condom on, and I'm back on top of her in seconds.

"Please, Chase. My body is aching for you to be inside it." She stares at me with pleading eyes.

I slide right in, and how wet she is catches me off guard. "Skyla, you feel incredible."

Skyla

Chase slides right in, filling me full. I feel desperate to be this close to him. His tongue probes my mouth as he thrusts into me repeatedly, answering my urgent plea. The ache I felt before is now a throbbing sensation, but it feels heavenly.

The lust he's unleashing on my body feeds my pleasure. I rake my nails down his back before I lift my hips, allowing him to bury himself deeper.

Each thrust grinds me into a space of sheer ecstasy. I open my eyes and Chase is giving me a burning stare.

"Keep your eyes on me, Skyla. I want to see your face again when you come."

His desire filled words and thrusts feed my pleasure until my trembling body climaxes, crashing around him. He plunges against my release before his body stiffens.

I feel the exquisite, powerful muscles along his body squeezing me tight as he erupts inside of me, letting out a harsh groan. He collapses, his face in my hair while heavy breaths of relief fan my neck.

"Every inch of you is fucking irresistible. You're mine, Skyla. All. Mine. I won't be able to let you go." He brushes kisses along my cheek and forehead while he strokes my hair.

We settle next to each other, and I curl up against him, hearing only our heavy breathing as I draw along the ripples of his abs with my fingertips.

"I don't want you to let me go, Chase, and that was the most exceptional orgasm ever." I rest on his chest, feeling happier and safer than I ever have in my life.

Chase

A blanket covers me when I wake up. It's Skyla's soft body draped across me, radiating so much warmth. I feel her chest moving above mine, her hair tickling my neck.

The magnitude of grief and loneliness I've felt for years is confirmed from the happiness I'm feeling today. I'm gently running my fingers through her hair as I glance at the clock and see that it's only one.

The doorbell rings. I debate on letting it go, but whoever it is rings the damn thing again. Surprisingly, I'm able to slide out from under Skyla without her waking.

She must be a heavy sleeper. She's now face down on my bed, looking alluring as ever with half her body out of the sheet. After slipping on my shorts, I go downstairs to the door.

"Hey, bro," Eric says.

"Figures I got out of bed for you."

"What's that supposed to mean, and why are you still in bed? It's after lunch, dude."

"Let's go out on the patio, and since when do you come to my front door?"

"Since I walked in on you groping Skyla." He's chuckling. "So, are things still going good between the two of you?"

In the past, I didn't hesitate to tell him there was a woman in my bed, but Skyla's special. It should be up to her if she wants him to know, so I need to get him out of here before she wakes up.

"I'm not pushing her away again. I really like her."

"I'm glad for ya, man. A little jealous but glad for both of you. I'm still going to be friends with her, so you're going to have to deal with that."

"I don't care if you're friends, but I can already tell that I'm going to be jealous with her. No one is taking her from me."

Eric gets his phone out. "Chill, bro, nobody's trying. I need to call her and see if she's coming down to the beach tomorrow before I forget."

Shit. He can't call her right now. "Why don't you do it later?"

"No. I want to see what she says about your sorry ass, anyway."

"Dammit, I said don't call her right now."

"I told you I'm going to be friends with her, Chase," he says as he looks at me with frustration.

"That's not why I don't want you to call her."

He stares at me for a few seconds before he smirks.

"She's in your damn bed right now."

"Yes, asshole, she's in my bed asleep, but I was trying to keep that to myself."

"Since when do you care if I know you have a woman over?"

"Skyla's not like any other woman, and you know that. I was going to let her tell you when she's ready."

Eric goes from a smile to an expression of concern.

"Don't let her go, man. Please, don't hurt her. She really likes you, too, and she was considering moving back to Cali when you were pushing her away. She said she couldn't take the loneliness here. I know she'll do it if you screw this up."

"I'm not going to hurt her or let her go anywhere. I already want to lock her in this house. I took her on the shark cage tour this morning, and it exhausted her."

He smirks again. "Yeah, I bet that's what wore her out. So, how was she?"

"What do you mean?"

"In bed."

"I'm not discussing that with you, and I can't believe you're asking when you two are friends."

"Damn. I never thought I'd see the day. You're already falling in love with her."

"I think it's time for you to leave. I'll tell her to call you." The door opens, and there stands Skyla, giving a bashful grin.

"Hi, Eric."

"Hi, Skyla."

I'm thankful she put her clothes back on before she came looking for me. She walks over, and I pull her into my lap. She fits perfect, and it's where she belongs.

"I'm happy you two are together, Skyla. He didn't want to tell me you were here, but I kept insisting on calling you, so he didn't have a choice. For once, Chase was being a gentleman," he says, laughing. "I was going to ask if we're still surfing tomorrow."

Skyla looks at me nervously and then to Eric.

"Yes, I really want to get back on my board."

"I'll come a little later. Let's make it nine in case you're shacked up with Mr. Grumpy here."

"He's not grumpy anymore." She gives me a gratifying smile before she leans down and plants a kiss on my neck. Time for Eric to leave, so I can take her sweet ass back to bed.

"You need to go before I get grumpy."

He shakes his head and smiles. "OK, I'll see you in the morning, Skyla. Try to convince him to get back out there while you're here."

Skyla looks at me after Eric is out of sight.

"Don't worry. I won't bug you about it. You'll do it when you're ready."

I gaze at her angelic face that's glistening from the sun. "Do you feel better after getting a nap?"

"Yes, but I didn't like waking up alone."

"I swear I didn't want to get out of bed, but Eric came ringing the doorbell. Your warm, naked body was wrapped up against me, so moving had not been my plan. Do you want some lunch?"

"Sure," she says before kissing my neck again.

"Stop that, or you're going to starve," I say before I stand up and carry her into the kitchen. She's giggling the whole way there.

We fix lunch together and sit across from each other at the table. Since my mom is from the mainland, I'm not a very traditional Hawaiian, but Skyla seems interested in soaking up all the knowledge she can.

I educate her more on the culture. I've never met anyone who appreciates life the way she does.

She locks eyes with me as she drinks from her glass of water, and it's the same look she had when she came back to clean that first week. It's a defiant look that is turning me on.

I walk over to her and pull her up from her chair. Leaning over, I whisper in her ear. "Do you want to go back to bed?"

She looks up at me seductively and nods. I swoop her up and carry her to my room. We remove each other's clothing, and I have to stop a few times in between to cup her face and kiss her passionately.

I love to kiss this woman. She owns me already, and I know this because she's the first person in my life whose needs I want to put before my own.

"Get in bed, Skyla. I'm taking my time pleasuring you, and you're going to let me."

One Riveting Day

Skyla

I struggle to slow my gasping breaths. Chase said he was going to take his time and pleasure me, and let me say he's a man of his word.

"I knew once I got a taste of you, it'd be addictive, and knowing I can drive you that crazy is only going to make me want to do it more," he says.

"No, I'll die if you do it again right now. It was so pleasurable that it was on the verge of painful."

Chase gets up and puts on a condom. Lying on top of me, his lips brush along my forehead, down to my temple and to my cheek.

"I want to make love to you, but I've never been that gentle before."

"Chase, you've already been gentle and sweet with me. I have no worries."

His lips curl up into a light smile before they claim my mouth. Our tongues twirl as he tenderly sinks into me.

We move together at a slow, sensual rhythm, relishing in the feel of the spellbinding friction we're creating.

Chase releases my lips and gazes at me with immense warmth in his dark eyes. Slightly increasing his tempo, he thrusts deeper inside of me, and I sense his struggle to go slowly. He pulls out slightly and drops kisses down my neck to my chest.

His tongue is taunting as it traces circles around my hardened nipple before he sucks it into his mouth, repeating several times on each breast.

A tingling spreads to my extremities, causing me to moan and arch against his wet, scorching mouth from the exquisite sensation. He groans and thrusts back into me.

"Holy shit, Skyla. You feel so warm and tight. I've never felt anything this insanely good before." His lips crash against mine, searing them with his satisfaction.

The tingling pleasure builds and builds each time he fills me full, climbing to an intensity that sweeps me to a shuddering orgasm.

My eyes close, and fingers delve into Chase's hair, grabbing on as I moan from the prolonged, pulsing ecstasy.

I feel his face bury into my neck, his body succumbing to its climax, jarring him above me. He lifts up and captures my mouth.

Shortly after, we're tangled up together, naked and warm, content from our lovemaking. I glide my fingertips down his arm before running them up the middle of his chest.

Patient lips graze along mine, mingling for a time as hands skim through hair and breaths collide. He lets my mouth go and gazes at me with sincerity.

"Skyla, I've been soaking in the feel of your skin, the way your lips tastes and how your touch causes every one of my nerves to ignite.

"I've never had sex without being drunk, high or coming off of it until today. I'm not numb or in oblivion, so I can hardly believe how amazing it felt and how good it was to take my time."

"You're the sweetest man, and I'm so grateful you gave us a chance."

"I want to ingrain in my mind the memory of how you feel, angel, so I can relive it every second you're not with me."

Minutes of memorizing and cherishing the other's needy body turn into hours, and I don't want night to fall.

A lovesick spell surrounds us like a shield, and I pray that nothing ugly permeates it. We're still tangled together as one with our eyes closed.

Our mouths and hands feel their way along the other's sultry skin, pleasure being our guide.

There are those few days in our lives that are so riveting and special that they'll stay with us forever. And when we think of them, we're taken right back, able to recall every touch, every smell, every sound. This is one of those days.

Chase

I don't want either of us to leave this bed–ever. My senses forgave me for the dormancy they were placed in, and now, I'm abusing them for pleasure and to bring Skyla as close to me as possible.

Her taste is like the sweetest lick of forbidden fruit. She was supposed to stay forbidden, but thank God she didn't allow that.

"So ... who wins?"

Her head is on my chest. She raises it to look at me.

"Wins what and who?" she asks.

"Me or the coconut-amaretto cream cake?" I try not to smirk but it's near impossible.

She rests her chin on her hands and gives me that cute ass smile. The one that makes me want to give her everything.

"Well ... the cake looks good, but it can't gaze at me with stunning, mysterious eyes." Skyla gives me an intense stare. "It smells decadent, but it can't breathe in my scent along my neck and hair, which sends chills through me."

She buries her face against my neck before planting kisses along it. "It tastes yummy, but it can't taste me, which feels phenomenal." Her tongue glides down the middle of my chest.

"Also, you look better, smell better and taste more delicious, so with that said ... you win by a long shot." Leaning up, Skyla plants a hot, arousing kiss on my lips.

Flipping her over, I straddle her and pin her hands by her head. I give a penetrating stare, letting her know that she's driving me insane. "You've done it now, angel, and it won't be slow and gentle this time."

A smile slowly spreads across her face.

"Swear?"

I shake my head. "You're an angel with horns."

She giggles, her chest vibrating below me. It's the happiest sound, and at this moment, I realize I can't live a day without Skyla.

***

More hours pass, and it's dark outside. We skipped dinner, but I'm just noticing since she's fed my appetite all day.

"I should go home. Will you take me?"

Her words are painful. I figured they were coming, but I've been hoping she'd fall asleep again and be here in the morning.

I don't want to spend another night alone in my bed. In actuality, I've been alone in it forever.

"You can stay here if you want." I want to beg, but I'm pathetic already. After how upset she became over me paying for all the seats on the boat this morning, I can't imagine how angry she'd be over the money I gave Hilda.

"I better go home. You were hardly speaking to me before a few days ago. I don't want you to feel like I'm crowding you."

"Tell me I haven't given you that impression."

"You haven't, but I don't want it to happen."

"I can assure you that it won't."

"My board's at home, and I have other stuff I'll need for tomorrow."

"OK, I'll take you." I move wayward strands of her silky hair away from her face and kiss her forehead.

I take the jeep in hopes she'll have a change of heart, and I can put her board in the back. Skyla plays with the back of my hair on the way to her house, and it makes me think of the night at the bar when I kept removing it. Now I'm pissed that she's going to.

"I can't fix lunch tomorrow since I'll be surfing, so I thought maybe all of us could go out to lunch after. Would you go with us?" she asks.

"Absolutely."

She kisses my cheek and gets out. This sucks. Now that I've given myself permission to be with her, it's going to be hard for me to accept that I can't have her whenever I want.

I've only ever been around women who would do what I tell them, so they could get their hands on money and drugs.

Skyla's independence is something that drew me to her, but it's also going to be the death of me. I want her like I've never wanted anything in my life.

No drug I've ever tasted on my tongue makes me feel as good as she does. I head back to my empty bed with the memories of a perfect day. A bed that smells like Skyla and sex.

Skyla

It takes all my strength not to stay the night with Chase. The day was perfect, so I want it to be just that, a day.

I'm falling in love with him, and I'm terrified I'm going to get hurt. His one hundred and eighty degree turn is a drastic one, so I'm paranoid.

He couldn't be sweeter or more attentive, and I hope with time I trust it completely. Chase is also used to getting his way, and I have to be sure not to lose myself. It would be easy with him.

His bossiness is adorable right now, how he's so protective. He has to see up front though that I'm still going to be my own person and make decisions for myself.

But damn, it pained me not to give him what he wanted tonight ... what I wanted, too.

A Shower of Reassurance

Chase

I get up early and make coffee. It became my drug once Bud died. I sit on the patio at eight o'clock in hopes that Skyla will come early and talk to me.

She insisted on walking, and I'm seeing that she's not going to do what I say just because she likes me.

I see her, and it perks me up way more than the damn coffee does. Shit, she looks good. She's wearing a black and pink rash guard with her little denim shorts.

"Hi," she says sweetly after she props up her board and sits down a bag.

Yes, that's something I can buy her, a new board. She walks over, and I pull her into my lap, kissing her neck.

"Good morning, baby." She smells like flowers again.

"If you don't care, I'm going to leave that bag of stuff here. I thought I could get a shower later."

"Of course. I'll even help if you need me to," I say with a chuckle before I kiss her neck again.

Turning her head, she kisses my cheek before hopping off my lap. "I'm going to go ahead and get into the water. It's been awhile, so I don't want to look like a complete amateur when the guys get here."

Skyla begins taking off her shorts, revealing black bikini bottoms. Watching her undress is like the Pavlov effect; I'm immediately horny. "Be careful."

"I will." She smirks and rolls her eyes before she goes down the steps. I watch her, and the farther out she paddles, the more panic fills me. I should be out there with her.

It's not long before I see the guys walk around the house onto the beach. They come to an abrupt stop when they recognize Skyla surfing. After a couple of minutes, they head my way.

"Bro, can you see her?" Eric asks as he and Andy come up the steps.

"She can surf," Andy says with amazement in his voice.

"I can see." I never take my eyes off her as fear consumes me. "Get out there with her," I say.

"You're worried about her. I see it all over your face. You obviously have nothing to worry about. The hot surfer chick would have to like your sorry ass," Eric says, sounding irritated before they walk away.

He might as well get over it. His chance with her is long gone. After a while, I go back inside. I can't take watching them any longer. I don't like that my guilt over Bud is affecting Skyla.

If I would surf, I'd be with her right now. I have to get back out there. It's not going to feel right surfing without Bud, but maybe surfing with Skyla will be the cure for that, too.

Skyla

It feels unbelievable to be back in the water. It's bittersweet since I didn't get a chance to surf off this island with Bud. The first couple of months after he died, I felt some responsibility for his death.

I'd say to myself that if I'd moved here sooner, it wouldn't have happened. I would've convinced him to clean up his act, but I finally acknowledged that being here wouldn't have been enough.

Maybe at first he would've behaved, but he'd dabbled with drugs since being a teenager, and Lee said his addiction had worsened.

He wouldn't have been able to stop without professional help. He was a thrill seeker, always looking for an adrenaline fix. Maybe that's what it felt like when he did drugs.

The guys and I decide to stop after a few hours.

"Skyla, you're really good. You should get into some competitions," Eric says as we walk up the steps.

We sit on the patio, trying to dry off some. Chase comes out and eyes me. He appears sad, but he also looks like he wants to eat me alive. I already know that look. He sits next to me and leans over to give me a kiss.

"You were killin' it out there," he says.

"Thanks. I'm usually better, but it's been a long time."

"Chick, you absolutely shred. You're already making us look bad, so you can't do better," Andy says.

"You're being nice."

Eric shakes water out of his golden blonde hair.

"No, we wouldn't tell you that if we didn't mean it. Did you forget where we're at? We've seen every skill level of surfing."

"Well, thanks guys. I'm going to go throw some clothes on, and we can get some lunch." I go inside and change into a tank and my denim shorts before putting my hair up into a messy bun. We pile into Chase's jeep and drive into town to eat.

All of us are in a great mood except for Chase. Mr. Moody is paying a visit. I might have to pressure him to get on that surfboard after all.

He misses it, and he's battling another internal struggle as to what to do about it. I can't believe he's punishing himself this much for his past mistakes.

We're eating, and I see Eric ogling a girl who looks younger than myself. I throw a French fry at him, hitting him right in the face. He jumps and looks at me.

"She doesn't look legal, but you should go find out. If she is, you can ask her out instead of drooling over her from this table," I say, laughing.

"That's it. In the ocean you're going next time, girl."

"Have you forgotten since this morning that I'll get in voluntarily?"

"Well, then I'll wait until that pretty hair of yours is fixed and toss your ass in."

I squeeze Chase's leg. "Tell him he can't throw me in."

"I don't have to. He knows that already," Chase says as he glares at Eric.

What's up with him? "Eric, I need to get my hot friend from California to move here. Then I can fix you up with her."

"Don't forget about me," Andy says.

"I don't have any more girlfriends worthy of dating you, Andy."

"Although that's a bummer, it's nice of you to say," he says with a wink.

"I need to get Brooke away from Rob, anyway. He treats her like shit. I sure don't miss being around that."

Eric gives me a boyish grin. "Make it happen. She won't want to return to the mainland after she visits here and gets a look at me."

"I'll work on that for ya." I throw another fry his way.

He looks at Chase. "Tell your girlfriend she can't throw French fries at me." He says it whiny like I did when I told Chase not to let him throw me in the ocean.

"I'm not his girlfriend." It's out of my mouth before I even think to sort out the consequences of my response. All three of them stop moving, and I know I have to look at Chase.

I glance to him, and he looks hurt and sad. He's already moody today, and I don't want to add to that.

"I mean, he hasn't asked me to be," I say quietly. It's the truth. He did say I was his yesterday. Is that the same thing?

Shit, if I'd taken time to process Eric's remark, I would've kept my mouth shut and let his comment pass on by. Things would not be weird like they are at this very moment.

Chase leans over and kisses my cheek.

"She's right; I haven't, but I think that needs to be remedied. Are all of you done eating?"

Eric and Andy are on their feet. It's visible they want out of here.

Chase

Andy and Eric leave as soon as we're back to my place, and I'm glad. I already don't like sharing Skyla's attention. Eric had to run his mouth and call her my girlfriend. I tried to rid the awkwardness, but I don't think it helped much.

I hadn't put any thought into labeling what we have between us. I know I don't want to be away from her for a second, and I sure as hell don't want her seeing anyone else. As soon as we're inside, Skyla takes my hand and leads me to the patio.

"Sit." She points to a chair.

I sit down, trying not to smirk. It's humorous when she's feisty. Curling up in my lap, she lays her head against my shoulder and strains to look up at me.

"I'm sorry I said that I'm not your girlfriend. It just came out. I think I didn't want you to feel pressured by what he said."

"It's fine, Skyla."

"What's up with you today? Don't tell me nothing. I can tell something's bothering you."

"A lot is happening. It was hard to watch all of you surf this morning, but I wasn't ready to get out there. Also, I don't want to share you. You seem so relaxed with my friends, especially Eric, and it bugs me.

"When I walked into that bar and saw you kiss his cheek while you were dancing with him, I was sure I'd lost my chance with you.

"I told you, I'm used to having my way and getting what I want. I want you more than I've ever wanted anything, Skyla, but I can't control how you feel or what you do. It's something I've never dealt with before."

"I have absolutely no desire for Eric, Andy or any other man to be anything more than a friend to me. I only want you, Chase."

She climbs out of my lap and takes my hand, pulling me out of the chair. After leading me straight up to my bathroom, she strips off her clothes without a word.

This woman is every man's fantasy, and she wants me. I undress and turn on the water in my shower. We get in, and she pushes me against the wall, thrusting her tongue into my mouth.

I groan against it and wrap my arms around her naked body. I feel the salt and sand on her skin, and it turns me on even more. She's sweet, strong, adventurous and spontaneous. She's wrapped in my arms, and I love her. I fucking love her.

I pick her up, and slide her right down onto my swollen cock. She's warm and wet inside, just like the outside of her red-hot body.

I turn to press her against the tiled wall before I repeatedly slam her down onto me. She cries out and digs her nails into my shoulders.

Her moans send lust roaring through my veins. Skyla's my new drug that I'll never quit. She's mine, and I won't let her go.

The pleasure builds, and I see in her flushed face that she's about to let go and give all of herself to me. It's erotic, and I can't hold out any longer.

Her muscles contract around me, and I pull out fast, suddenly realizing I don't have a condom on. She got me so worked up that I didn't even think about it. Our bodies shake, and I feel on fire once again.

I lean my head against her forehead and feel her labored breaths against my face. "I don't deserve to feel this good, and I don't deserve you," I say.

"Shut up," she says through a gasp, barely able to speak. "Just shut up and make me feel that good every day." Capturing my mouth again, she slides out of my arms and onto her feet.

After drying off, we lie in bed, and Skyla falls asleep in my arms. I imagine it's from the surfing and sex. I smile over how cute it is that her little body gets worn out so easily.

It makes me want to take care of her. She showed me how strong her feelings are for me, and I know I have to let her be close to my friends. There's nothing for me to worry about.

Relinquishing the control I want will keep her with me. I'm trying to learn this lesson. For over nine months, I've been trying to repent for all my selfish mistakes. She's the sweet angel that's going to guide me the rest of the way there.

***

After a couple of hours of peaceful sleep, I decide to go to the store to get something to fix for dinner. I leave Skyla a note on the island in the kitchen.

A Love Note and a Boat

Skyla

I wake up alone again in Chase's bed. He owes me now. Missing him already, I slip on some clothes and walk downstairs. There's a note on the island.

Baby, if you read this, then that means you're out of my bed, and I'll soon be disappointed that I can't sneak back in to curl up next to you. Please forgive me. I promise to wake up with you tomorrow if you'll stay with me tonight. Hint. I've gone to the store. Be back soon. By the way ... I love you, Skyla.

His precious words take my breath away. I stand frozen in his kitchen, tears filling my eyes. His love this soon is unexpected, and I don't think he could've told me in a sweeter way.

I stare at his note and read it over and over for several minutes until the doorbell rings. I open it to a Hawaiian lady holding flowers.

"Hi, can I help you?" I ask.

She looks at me with a stunned expression.

"Hello, is Mr. Kalani here?"

"No, ma'am, but he should be back soon."

"I'm Hilda. I was Chase's housekeeper."

"Oh, please come in."

She walks straight toward the kitchen, so I follow her with a smile. It's obvious she's used to being in his home. After sitting down the basket arrangement of flowers, she turns to me and smiles. We stand for a moment in silence.

"I'm sorry. I didn't introduce myself. I'm Skyla, Chase's ... girlfriend." He loves me, so I think it's safe to say.

"How wonderful," she says with enthusiasm, entwining her fingers and holding them up in front of her chest. "Chase has been alone way too long. How did you two meet?"

"Actually, I came here to clean. I was filling in for you. I wasn't supposed to come back, but he told me you quit, so he asked the agency to send me. I think he liked me already." I smile and feel my face flush.

That was more information than she needed to hear, but I'm still gushing inside from his note and want to scream to the world that he loves me.

Throwing her head back, she laughs loudly, seeming genuinely delighted.

"Can I ask what's so funny?"

"I should've known Chase had another motive, but that doesn't change what he did for me, and I owe him tremendously. That's what the flowers are for, a very overdue thank you.

"I've been taking care of my husband, who had hip surgery, so I haven't had a chance to bring him a gift until today."

"Oh, did you have to quit your job to take care of your husband?"

She smiles warmly and reaches out to squeeze my hand. "No dear, Chase graciously gave me enough money to retire. It couldn't have come at a better time. It's the only reason I could stay home and take care of my husband.

"I should've known there was another reason he was trying to get me out the door. He must really like you. I can tell you're a good girl, so I'm glad you came into his life.

"He's been lonely for a long time, and it's been breaking my heart for months, especially since he's made so many good changes." She laughs once again and shakes her head.

"He paid a fortune to see your pretty face once a week, so I'm glad it's progressed quickly. Please tell him I was here and that I miss him. I need to get back to my husband."

I feel faint as I follow her to the front door. She hugs me tight before she leaves, and I stand in Chase's foyer, holding his sweet note, wondering what other secrets he holds. Surely, he didn't give her money only so he could see me once a week. I mean, we just met.

Every emotion washes over me. I don't know whether to feel flattered, embarrassed or angry. I love this man, and it's scaring me. Something about this isn't adding up. I go out on the patio and curl up in one of the lounge chairs.

The sun, my comforting friend, soaks into me, crowding out some of the vulnerability that's seizing me, causing me to question the astounding week I've had with Chase.

Love and fear gush from me in the form of tears as the unfaltering strength normally carried with me is nowhere to be found. Wet drops hit my note, so I fold it neatly and hold it against my chest.

No matter what happens, I'll keep it forever. It's the sweetest words ever given to me.

Chase

I walk into the kitchen and set my bags on the counter. There are flowers on my island, and I wonder where they came from. My heart pounds in my chest when I see the note's gone.

Thinking she might be in my bed, I run upstairs. I'm ready to hold her again. She's not there, and I can't find her in the house. Did my words scare her away?

I'm beginning to feel sick as I run to the glass doors off the kitchen. Maybe she's on the patio or beach.

Her cries flood my ears the second I step outside. She's curled up in a ball on the lounge chair, sobbing uncontrollably. I sit at the end of the long chair and pull her into my lap.

"Oh god, Skyla. What's wrong?"

She buries her face into my chest and continues to cry hard. As she struggles to get her breath, I see that she's not going to be able to speak any time soon.

I pick her up, carrying her inside and to bed. It might be the last place she wants to be, but I need to hold her.

Her sobbing subsides, and she whimpers against my chest as I stroke her hair. Her harsh breathing finally eases, and I'm so damn grateful she's calming down. I have to know what's upset her and if I'm the cause.

"Skyla, please sit up and talk to me. I'm worried about you. You need to tell me what happened. Where did the flowers come from? Is it my note that upset you?"

She moves off of my lap, and I see that her blue eyes are swollen and encased in redness. I hurry and grab her tissues from the bathroom.

When I sit next to her, I see her holding my note, running her fingers over it as if she's trying to smooth out the wrinkles.

"Your note. It's ... so sweet. It surprised me. I never expected for you to love me and definitely not this soon."

"That can't be why you're this upset. What happened?" I ask desperately.

"Hilda came by. She brought the flowers as a thank you gift."

Shit. "I'm sorry, Skyla. I don't know what she told you, but from how upset you are, I'm guessing she told you what I did."

"How much did you give her?"

"I'm not trying to be rude, but I think that's personal."

Her eyes fly open wide and fill with anger.

"Under normal circumstances I would never pry, but I feel I have a right to know since it has to do with me."

"I can't tell you. You were upset with me for buying all the spots on the boat, so I know you'll be even more upset over this. Does it really matter?

"I didn't do it only to see you. I mean, I wouldn't have thought to help her if it wasn't for wanting to see you again, but I still did it for her, too. You were the main reason but not the only one."

"Tell me, or I'm leaving."

I hang my head. I'm embarrassed and also scared she'll walk out that door and not come back because she thinks I'm sick in some way.

This amount of money will seem like so much more to her than it does to me, but she's leaving if I don't tell her. I look up and gaze into her cautious eyes.

They're untrusting at the moment, and I hate it. I'll do whatever it takes to fix this. I'll tell her how long I've been watching her at the beach if I have to.

"I gave her a hundred thousand dollars."

She bursts into tears again and starts to hurry off my bed in the direction away from me. I stretch across the bed, and right when her feet hit the ground, I grab her arm.

"Please, Skyla. I'm begging you not to leave. I can explain. Please, give me a chance to explain."

She hesitates but then climbs back on the bed, scooting to the head of it. Leaning her head back against it, she blows her nose.

I sit in front of her and tuck some strands of hair behind her ear, noticing they're wet.

"When did you decide to give her the money?" she asks between jarring breaths.

I close my eyes. This keeps getting worse.

"The first day you came to clean."

"I don't understand, Chase. You'd just met me the night before. You didn't even know me. It's bizarre. Then to push me away repeatedly makes no sense after giving away that kind of money. You didn't even know for sure you'd see me again."

"I need to tell you something, and I hope you'll understand. I swear I wasn't trying to stalk you."

Skyla looks at me with apprehension as I take her hand. I stare into her eyes, determined to show her how long and how much I've loved her.

"A few months ago, I was sitting on my back steps. An attractive woman, barefoot and in a sundress, came walking by. It was dark and unsafe for her to be on the beach alone.

"I watched as she stared out toward the ocean before she buried her feet in the sand. She looked sad, and I wanted more than anything to know her thoughts. I couldn't get her out of my head and worried if she got home safely.

"I was on my steps the next night when she returned, and I was relieved to see she was OK but frustrated that she was once again alone on the beach. I became fascinated by the way she played in the sand as she walked by my house.

"I waited every night that I was home, which was most, to see if she returned. I'd feel empty and worried when she didn't.

"I did this for three months, and then one night, when I thought some guys were intending to hurt her, I decided to intervene. That's when I got to see her up close and hear her sweet voice. She was beautiful and strong.

"I didn't feel I deserved a conversation with her, so I only planned to continue watching her on the beach, but the very next day, she appeared in my home.

"After spending that time with her and seeing how sweet she was, I was desperate to be near her. I felt so drawn to her and was willing to do anything to keep her in my life."

Skyla listens, and halfway through my story, she weeps, clinging to every word, knowing it's about her. Staring at me for seconds that feel like forever, she finally crawls into my lap and curls herself against me. I hold her in silence for several minutes.

"I'm overwhelmed. Only men in my family have loved me, and they're expected to, but you chose to watch me night after night. You chose to do whatever you could to see me and keep me safe. You *chose* to love me.

"How could I be angry at you for that? I feel like the most loved woman on earth, and I can't imagine a more touching story. I'm sorry that I made you tell me, but I'm grateful you did."

She straddles my lap and kisses me tenderly, but her touch to my skin is like electricity.

"I love you, Chase."

We undress each other and fall into bed as our hands and mouths begin to do as they did the day before. They trail, linger, stroke and caress.

Most men would say I need to stop being such a girl, but screw them. This is foreplay at its finest, and I think it feels fucking fabulous.

"Chase," she says.

"Yes, angel."

"Can I spend the night?"

"Yes. I was going to beg this time," I say with relief.

We miss dinner again, and Skyla stays right where she belongs for the night, wrapped safely in my arms.

Skyla

Sunlight shines through the long row of windows and wakes me. I'm twisted with Chase's body, and it feels wonderful. He's here this time.

My eyes hurt, and I can feel that they're still swollen. I'm embarrassed for how hard and long I cried yesterday. I thought he didn't like me in the beginning, but he really did.

My stomach knots when I think of the times I was out with Eric. It had to have been painful for Chase since he'd watched me for months.

I want to go make him breakfast, but after last night, I think he'd panic if I wasn't in his bed. The sunlight is shining on his hair, making it appear even more lustrous, and I can't resist running my fingers through it.

He lets out a little sigh and pushes himself closer to me. After a couple of minutes, he opens his eyes.

"Good morning," I say, smiling.

He smiles and pulls me tight against his side.

"It's a good morning since you're still here. When you told me you had several days off in a row, I planned a surprise for today, so you need to cancel whatever you have going on."

"I was going to do laundry," I say, giggling.

"What fun is that?"

"You can't surprise me again. They're stressing me out."

"This one will be fun and relaxing. We're going to stay the night on my boat."

"So, you decided this on your own? What if I say no?"

"I'll beg. I'm not above it with you," he says as he rolls onto me. "We better get moving. I'm looking forward to seeing you prance around in a bikini without there being other spectators. Well, except for the crew, but I'll throw them overboard if I catch them."

"You have a crew?"

He gazes at me, and his expression turns serious.

"I'm sorry I didn't tell you about Hilda. I didn't know how."

"I know, but I can't believe you spent that kind of money so you could see me once a week. It's insane, but I'm glad it helped Hilda out, anyway."

"You have no idea how much it was worth it."

I gaze back at his brown eyes that become a little less mysterious every day. "My brother will be pleased to know I'm seeing someone who's good to me. I have a track record for picking losers."

"How often do you talk to him?"

"I've only spoken to him a couple of times since he left. We write letters to each other. He worries about me being here alone, but I wrote to him last week, letting him know I've made friends.

"He's trying to come home around Christmas. I'll be twenty-one and can finally have my trust fund from my dad's insurance policy.

"My brother's the executor, so it will take months of paperwork back and forth between him and an attorney if he can't come home.

"I need it to pay for school, so he's trying hard to get leave for a couple of weeks. It'll be during the holidays, which will be nice, too. I can't wait for you to meet him."

"As sweet and pretty as you are, I bet he's protective as hell."

"He acts that way when we're together, but we've hardly seen each other for a couple of years. He talked me into moving here, so he could keep an eye on me, but then he got his orders to leave.

"We'll eventually be here together since he plans on staying in Hawaii when he gets out of the Army."

"I'll have to share you with another man. I don't like it already."

"You're funny. What's it going to take for you to see how much of your attention I want?"

"Let's get up before we end up here all day."

"I have no complaints about being in this bed. Well, actually ..."

"What is it, Skyla?" He looks at me with concern.

"I hate thinking of all the women that have been in this bed." I bite my bottom lip, nervous that he'll be upset with me.

He smiles. "You're the only woman that's been in this bed. I bought a new one when I got out of rehab. I didn't want anything in this house that was tainted from my past. It was made for you, baby." He chuckles and plants a big, wet kiss on my cheek.

I can't help but grin at him. He's too stinkin' cute.

"I want to make love to you on my damn boat, so get your cute ass moving." He gives me a sly grin before he climbs off of me.

***

"Chase Kalani! This is not a boat. It's a damn yacht!"

"OK, maybe a small one," he says as he helps me step on board. He thinks his surprises are funny. I tried to surprise him in the shower yesterday, and I think I succeeded, but I can't compete with this.

While he's on deck speaking to a male crew member, he tells me to go inside and look around. There's a kitchen with stainless steel appliances on this thing! I run back up the stairs to the deck.

He stops speaking and looks at me with a smirk.

"What is it, angel?"

He must see that goofy grin on my face again.

"You have a kitchen." I'm such a dork. I say it like he wouldn't know. Now, the man he's speaking with is smirking.

"Yeah, there's a bed in there, too," he says with a wink.

Shit, now I'm embarrassed, so I hurry back inside. I look around, and sure enough, there's a bed in its own room. This is not like any boat I've ever seen. This is a luxurious house on water.

Unbelievable. I've really lived a simple, sheltered life. It has a bathroom, a bar and a small living room with a couch. There are two flat screen TV's, and the woodwork throughout is remarkable.

I'm staring at the kitchen stove, chewing on my thumbnail. For some reason, I find the fact that there's a kitchen on this boat fascinating. I feel arms wrap around me, and Chase whispers in my ear.

"I'd prefer you be more interested in the bed than the kitchen."

I turn around. "You have a stove, a refrigerator and a sink."

"And a bed." He pulls me into his arms and kisses on my neck. He obviously has sex on the brain.

"So, do I make you this horny, or is it the fact that you own a yacht with a bed in it?"

He barely removes his lips from my neck.

"Mostly you, but I can't lie; the bed does it for me, too."

His hands work their magic, moving up under my sundress until his fingers slide into my bikini bottoms and into me. I lean against him from the immediate pleasure, already feeling my legs wanting to buckle.

"I want you right now, Skyla."

I remember there are other people onboard and pull away from him. "You have other people here. What if they walk in?"

He frowns. "That won't happen. I can assure you."

The next thing I know, he's picking me up and carrying me to the bedroom, using his foot to shut the door behind us. In one swift move, he has my dress off.

His eager hands and mouth are everywhere, and as always, it feels amazing. I try to get his clothes off, which is challenging since his hands are on the move. I can't help but giggle.

He stops and gives me a piercing stare.

"I'm sorry, but I'm trying to get your clothes off, and you're not making it easy," I say.

"Get into bed, Skyla."

I climb in and watch him dig through a duffle bag. He holds a condom wrapper between his teeth while he takes off his clothes. I try not to laugh, but his urgency is humorous.

I haven't seen him like this before. My bikini is still on, so I start to remove my bottoms, and when they're halfway down my legs, he yanks them off.

"Roll over," he says.

Oh, my. We're not making love. I feel the pull of the strings on my bikini top before he slides it right out from under me.

He's on top of me, holding himself up by his forearms. He moves my long hair before he's kissing and nibbling the back of my neck.

I know any second he's going to be inside me, and my body is aching for it. He reaches around and grabs hold of my breast, massaging it in his large hand. I lean up until I'm on my hands and knees, giving him easy access to every part of my needy body.

He growls, squeezing my breast harder as he thrusts into me. The forward movement continues, and the friction against my sensitive flesh is mind-blowing.

His hand moves from my breast to the back of my hair. I feel it being gathered and twisted around his wrist before he gently tugs it.

I've never imagined wanting my hair pulled, but it sends a prickling sensation across my scalp that only spreads farther throughout my body, and it feels surprisingly great. I close my eyes as the pleasure builds from his thrusts.

The most glorious sensation rushes to my core as I see sparks of white. With one hard thrust and light yank of my hair, Chase pulses deep inside of me, squeezing my ass with his other hand as he climaxes.

He growls loudly and collapses on top of me. We lie breathless and stuck together for a few minutes before he moves next to me. I'm still on my stomach, my head facing him.

"Your ass is spectacular, and I know this because I had the best view." His face is inches from mine.

I giggle. "I hope you enjoyed it because that's as close as you're getting to it."

His eyebrows raise, and he smirks. "You're a dirty girl. That thought wasn't there, but it is now." He shakes his head. "My angel with horns."

I giggle more. "That was erotic. Everything you do is over the top, and I don't know how I'm going to surprise you."

"You surprise me every minute, Skyla."

Chase

I just fucked her doggy style while pulling her hair, and she's telling me how erotic it was while giggling at the same damn time.

She's a piece of work. The finest I've ever touched or tasted. An exquisite piece of fine art that I plan to have on display in my home forever.

I make love to her the rest of the times on the yacht, and I enjoy it. I have more time to touch her silky skin, and I get to be inside of her longer. It's fantastic.

Not to mention that I get to see a gushing smile from her gorgeous face after. She loves it when I'm gentle with her, and I'll do more of anything she wants to keep her with me.

All we do on the yacht besides make love is eat and lounge on deck. I spend a lot of time staring at her flawless body in tiny bikinis and decide that she needs more of them. She also needs lingerie. That's a sight I'm craving, too.

***

She refuses to stay the night, so I'm unhappy when I take her home. The good news is tomorrow's Tuesday, and she'll be over to clean, so I'll get four hours with her.

I don't feel right having her do it now that we're dating, but she insists that it's a way for her to get paid and see me at the same time.

Although, she laid down the law that she won't sleep with me while she's here working since she's getting paid during that time. Some of her morals are funny but refreshing.

A Secret Kept

Skyla

I can hardly sleep without him, waking up constantly throughout the night. I had no idea being in love would feel this good and scary all at the same time.

Knowing how easily he could crumble up my heart in his hand is unnerving. I'm trusting him more every day, so that's what I'm hanging onto.

Chase is insisting I bring some things over to leave at his house, so to appease him I gather some toiletries, a bikini and an extra change of clothes.

I'm literally right down the street from him, but I see it will make him feel more secure that I'm his and that I'm not going anywhere.

I guess he has the same fears I do. I finish the other homes I clean and walk to his place.

"Aloha, baby. Get your butt in here, so I can hug you." He's grinning, and it tickles me to see how enthused he is.

We stand in his foyer, making out like teenagers until I feel his erection. "OK, I have to work," I say, pulling away from him.

He kisses my neck. "No, I'll say you did. You can exert your energy in other ways."

"No, Chase. We talked about this, and you're failing the first day."

He scowls and groans like a child. "Fine, I'll let you work. You should give the agency notice that you're quitting, and let me take care of you.

"Then I can spend more time with you before you're busy with school. I don't want you having to work this hard."

"Chase, we just got together. I can't give up my job and let you support me. That's crazy. You know I'm not that kind of person."

"I'll let you get to work, and we can discuss it later."

I sigh. "OK." I can't argue with him right now, or I'll never get done today. He's not going to drop this.

It takes about an hour longer for me to finish cleaning since Chase wants us to talk and make out about every twenty minutes. It's cute and makes me feel loved. I can't be upset with this man.

"You'll be satisfied to hear that I brought a few of my things over." I hold up my bag.

"Good, your things belong in this house. I'll make room for them in my dresser."

"That's silly. You have a ton of rooms, so I'll put them in a dresser in one of the spare bedrooms."

"OK, and while you're doing that, I'll fix us something to eat." He gives me another heated kiss, and I know what's on his agenda for the rest of the day.

I go into one of the spare rooms and open a drawer. It has extra towels in it, so I open another one. It's full of loose pictures.

Right on top is one of Chase when he was young. It's so obvious it's him. He's smiling, and it makes me think about how happy he probably was before his parents died.

I pick up another photo of him, and then I see it. I'm paralyzed, unable to move or breathe. I tremble as I pick up the picture. It's Bud.

My Daniel. My Bud.

Why? Why is his picture in Chase's home? I sit on the bed and stare at it. He's in swim trunks, holding his board and smiling.

Think, Skyla. Think, think. Which one of Bud's friends is Chase? He's wealthy and has a house on the beach.

Oh. My. God. He's King.

Bud's best friend, King. He thinks he's responsible for Bud's death. This explains everything.

I have to get out of here!

I need time to figure out what to do. I jump as I hear Chase coming down the hall. After shoving the photos in the drawer, I take a deep breath.

I'm not a liar, but I have no choice right now. I could lose him if I don't think this through.

"Baby, what are you doing?"

"Sorry, um ... I'm not feeling well. I need to go home."

"What's wrong? You're really pale."

"My stomach's bothering me. I don't want you to catch something if I'm getting a virus."

"No way, angel. Let me take care of you. We've been kissing, so I'm already exposed, anyway. I don't know how good I'll do, but I want to take care of you."

"No, I'd feel better in my own bed." Damn, the look on his face. I've hurt him.

"Please, Skyla. Get in my bed."

"I might throw up."

"I don't care. I want to take care of you," he says more forcefully as he picks me up.

"I'll compromise. I'll stay here for a while, but I'm going home later. I have to work tomorrow, so I want to be there."

"We'll see." He carries me to his room.

I *am* sick at my stomach. It's twisted into knots. I see Chase differently now, loving him even more. Should I tell him who I am? He covers me up after placing me in his bed.

"What can I get you for your stomach?"

"Would you go to the store and get me some ginger ale or Sprite?"

He points his finger at me. "Sure, but you stay in this bed. Don't leave, or I'll drag your ass back here."

"OK, I won't."

He kisses my forehead, and I can see it pains him to leave me. I don't know how I'll get out of this house today. My heart's pounding, and I'm sweating.

Eric and Andy!

They're Shooter and Brody. From Bud's stories, Eric has to be Shooter. This is insane. I found Bud's friends that he talked about all the time.

I should've known it was a possibility since I'm near where he died, but they don't go by their nicknames. I feel foolish that I didn't piece it all together.

Shit, of course, that's why Chase doesn't surf. I recall all the emails Bud and I exchanged about his friends.

Chase and I fell in love on our own. Bud wanted King and Nixie together and it happened. Grief over Daniel spills from me in the form of tears.

He's been in this house countless times, and I feel like he's here. I feel like I'm home.

Anguish washes over me as I think of the suffering Chase has put himself through. It wasn't his fault. How can he not see that? He even got clean like Bud wanted.

Shit, I mentioned Bud at the bar, so Eric and Andy have to know. How could they not tell us? I have to talk to Eric. Chase returns and brings me something to drink.

"Skyla, what's wrong? I can tell you've been crying."

Right now I need to be close to him. The concern and love he has for me is written all over his face.

"I'm not feeling good, and I'm a little emotional. When I feel bad, I miss my mom." That's the truth. I truly wish my mom was here to tell me what to do. "Will you lie in bed with me?" I ask.

His eyes light up. We're such alike, desperate to be loved and needed.

"Of course." He climbs into bed, and I try to fall asleep. I need the time to pass, so I can talk to Eric.

***

I wake up in Chase's warm arms. Sitting up, I glance at the clock and see we've been asleep a couple of hours.

I lie facing him and stare at his captivating face. What if the guilt is too much for him and he pushes me away? I won't let him. I won't.

Desperation and fear weave through the contentment and love that fills me, and I feel a need to be even closer to him.

"Chase." I run my fingers through his satiny hair until he opens his eyes.

"Are you OK? Do you need something?"

"I feel better." I nuzzle my face into his neck and start kissing it. "Chase, will you please make love to me? I need to be closer to you."

He rolls over onto me and shows me how much it means to him to know he's needed and loved.

Chase

I roll off of Skyla and pull her to me. She's different today. For the first time since I met her on the beach, she seems ... scared. Not of me but of something.

"That was a nice surprise," I say.

"I love you, Chase."

"I love you, too. Are you sure you feel better?"

"Yes, and I should get home."

"Please stay with me, so I'll know you're OK."

"I need to go home, and I promise I'm doing better. If I get feeling bad, I know where I can find you." She gives me a faint smile.

I can't figure it out. She wanted to be close to me, but now she wants to leave. "OK, but I'm taking you."

"I figured as much. I'll come see you tomorrow evening." She kisses my cheek and gets up to dress.

I drive her home, and before she gets out of the Jeep, I take her hand. "Skyla, I want you to know that what's mine is yours. I don't want you to ever think you can't stay over."

"I know I can stay. You're a great person, and I won't stop telling you until you believe it, too. I'll see you tomorrow. I love you."

Eric

It's eight o'clock when I get a text from Skyla. She always calls, so it seems odd.

Skyla: *Could you come over? I need to talk to you ... without Chase.*

Damn, what's this about? Does she know? Maybe it has nothing to do with that.

Me: *OK, I'll be over in thirty.*

My stomach tightens as I make the drive to Skyla's. I hate not knowing what I'm walking into. If she knows, will she be pissed at me? I park in her driveway, my stomach aching even more as I walk to the door.

"Eric, come in."

"What's up, chick?" She stares at me for several seconds and begins sobbing. Shit. Don't cry. I hate it when women cry. "Skyla, what's wrong?"

She throws her arms around my neck, so I hug her. Did Chase already hurt her? "Did Chase fuck up already? Do I need to kick his ass?"

She lets me go and gazes at me, tears trailing her cheeks. "We're Shooter and Nixie," she says, barely above a whisper.

Shit, she knows!

"I–I'm sorry I didn't say anything. I haven't known what to do. Please, Skyla, don't be upset with me. I've been trying to protect you both."

"Why? Why didn't you tell us?"

"Look, Chase cares about you. You know that, but he blames himself for Bud's death. If I told, he would've pushed you away because of his guilt."

"You're right. He would've then. He was already pushing me away."

"Andy and I freaked. Discovering you're Nixie messed us up. I was afraid Chase would find out and not recover. He finally seemed alive again, and Bud wanted you together. You're my friend, too, and I was afraid you'd move away."

"So, what were you going to do? You had to know Chase and I would eventually talk about Bud."

"Andy and I prayed that by the time you two found out, your relationship would be able to survive it. Does Chase know?"

"No. I found a picture of Bud at his house today. I couldn't believe it, but then after thinking about it, I couldn't believe I didn't discover it on my own.

"You, Chase and Andy are the way Bud described, and I've thought several times how lucky I am to have found guys that remind me of Bud and his friends."

"You can't tell him yet, Skyla. You've only officially been together, what a week? I believe he'll still push you away. He's nuts about you, but he still thinks he doesn't deserve you."

"I'm not a deceitful person. I don't know if I can keep this from him. He might hate me later if I do."

"First, he has to believe Bud's death is not his fault," I say.

"I can't convince him of that if I can't talk to him about it." She paces around in front of me. "He told me he loves me."

"He said that already?" I'm shocked. I knew he was falling for her, but I had no idea he cared for her that much already.

"Did you know he used to watch me on the beach before we met?"

"What do you mean?"

"The first three months I was here, I would go to the beach near Chase's house almost every night since it's near where Bud died.

"Lee showed me the spot when I moved here. Chase waited on his steps to watch me and claims he did it the entire three months. I never knew he was there.

"That's why he was around when Troy and his friends approached me on the beach. He said he always worried about me being out in the dark. It's as if it was meant to be, like Bud had him watching out for me."

"He never told me."

"He also paid Hilda a hundred thousand dollars to retire, so I'd be the one cleaning his house."

I shake my head and laugh hard. "He's so rotten. He goes to great lengths to get what he wants. That means he'd already fallen for you then. I know you've figured out how passionate he is, but it can be his worst enemy at times."

"What I'm trying to say, Eric, is that he's cared about me longer than you think, so maybe he wouldn't push me away."

"Skyla, you don't know how bad things were. I almost lost him along with Bud. There were many days that Andy and I didn't think he'd be alive when we went to his house."

"I don't know what to do. I can't lose him," she says as she begins to cry again. I take her into my arms and hold her.

"I still can't believe you're Nixie, and you're really here."

"I miss Bud, Eric."

I don't let her go. "I miss him, too, but I feel like he's with us when I'm near you, Skyla. You're so friendly and exude happiness like he did." Dammit, now I'm crying. None of us should have to deal with this shit.

She pulls away from me and sees my tears. I go to wipe them away, but she beats me to it.

"I won't say a word. He has to love me more and be with me longer to ensure he can't walk away from what we have. I can't risk something happening to him from the guilt he feels."

"Thank you, Nixie." I hug her one more time.

"You like calling me that, don't you?"

"How could I not? You're Bud's Nixie. Actually, I have no idea what I'll call you, but it has to be Skyla for now."

She frowns. I know it's going to be hard for her to keep this from Chase.

"If he ever brings Bud up, then I'm telling him the truth," she says adamantly.

"OK."

"Thank you for being such a good friend, Eric."

I point my finger at her. "I'll see you later. Call me if you think you're going to crack. Don't tell him without calling me first. Maybe I can be there to help smooth it over." I go out the door and inhale a deep breath. The future's scary.

Back on Board

Skyla

I've refused to sleep over at Chase's for the last two nights. I told him I'd only stay on the weekends, and he's been pouting ever since.

I'm afraid he's going to get tired of me, and I don't want to gradually move in with him. If we ever move in together, I want it to be because he's put real thought into it and asks me.

I haven't shared those thoughts with him, but I have to admit that if he asked, I'd say yes. That's moving really fast, but I love him, and I miss him the second we're apart.

I'll have to tell him that I'm Nixie for sure then. Since he seemed so upset with me last night for not sleeping over, I decide to go see him early this morning before I head to work.

He doesn't answer the door when I knock, so I go around back to find he's not on the patio, either. It's only seven, so I wonder if he might actually be sleeping in.

He seldom sleeps, and I think it's from anxiety. It's not long before I need to go to work, so I decide to sit on his back steps on the beach instead of going back home.

I brought pastries and fresh pineapple, so I get it out and eat. Staring at the water, I see one male surfer, and he's awesome.

While eating my breakfast I watch him. I'm wondering if I should call and wake up Chase. I want to see him and be sure he isn't sulking too badly.

As I stare at the surfer some more, it hits me like a ton of bricks. I think it's Chase. Oh, please be him. My heart races, and I can't keep the smile off my face. The more I stare, the more I can tell from his body that it's him.

I watch in amazement. He's unbelievably good, and I can't help but think that maybe I played some part in him surfing again. He's becoming whole.

I should leave. He might not want me to see him, and I don't want him to stop, so I hurry and pack up my stuff. I quickly walk to my car, feeling so much joy in my heart. I'll make sure we survive this.

Chase

This is where I belong. Damn, I've missed this. It feels right, so I know I'm doing better. Skyla has filled the empty space inside of me that was created from so many losses in my life.

I hope that Mom, Dad and Bud can somehow see her and know how right she is for me.

I'll be able to surf with her now, and I'm damn excited about it. Eric didn't have to work this morning, so I told him to come at eight to surf.

I needed to go it alone at first, but now that I see him paddling out, I'm glad he's here.

Eric

Chase called me last night and asked if I had to work this morning. He wanted us to surf. I told him I was free, but I lied.

I called my assistant right after we hung up and told her to move my morning appointments when she got into the office today.

I wasn't about to miss a chance to surf with Chase, and I didn't want to take a chance on him changing his mind.

"Bro, I can't tell you how awesome it is to see you out here," I say, sitting on my board.

"It's time, and I owe it all to Skyla. She showed me that I needed to get off the guilt trip."

"I've been telling you that for almost a year."

"Yeah, but you're a dude. You don't have a gorgeous face or tight body that's trying to convince me, and she's found some creative ways to be persuasive. I've let her share all of them with me, too," he says, chuckling.

"I see King's crude humor is back, and I think it's a good thing."

Fuck, why did I call him that?

"Man, I'm sorry. It just came out. I guess because this is reminding me of old times."

"It's time to hear it again. It makes me feel like he's here, so it's cool. Just don't call me that around Skyla. I haven't told her about Bud yet, so I don't want her asking why you call me that. This rides for you, Bud," he says as he goes to drop in.

Bud would say that Chase seemed like a king with his fortune and mansion on the beach. He also joked that Chase thought he was king of this part of the beach and ocean. He was right about that one.

Our nicknames have been too painful to hear, especially for Chase. Bud earned his from everyone becoming his buddy. He was too damn nice and funny for anyone not to like him.

Damn, I miss him. It's cool to know I can call Chase "King" again. He's been King for years now. I guess it's still too upsetting for him to tell Skyla about Bud.

They're getting closer every day though, and now that they're both surfing again, it's just a matter of time. Guilt would swallow King whole and not spit him out if he knew he was sleeping with Bud's very own Nixie.

We finish up surfing and sit on the patio.

"Man, I have to meet Skyla's brother in a couple of months. I don't know how I feel about that. She said he's protective of her, but she thinks he's going to love me.

"She's wishful thinking. What guy really loves the man who's banging his baby sister? It's cute, but damn, she's naïve. Her twenty years of age shows sometimes."

I gulp. I don't know what he said after saying that he'll meet Skyla's brother. Lee, or "Rock" as we call him, wanted someone to blame for his cousin's death, so he chose King.

Most people who didn't want to admit that Bud was flawed blamed him. It was easy to do since King was taking responsibility for Bud's death himself.

Most people have no idea that it was Bud who got him hooked on hard drugs, not the other way around. Since Chase had the dough and the house they could party at, everyone assumed he was the bad influence.

I tried to take up for King, but he stopped me and wouldn't let me say a word. He said there was no way to save his reputation without tarnishing Bud's. He was right.

We didn't hang out with Rock that often. Aside from him disliking King over the drug use, he didn't like that Bud had gotten so close to Andy, Chase and me, so he was a prick when he was around us.

Rock mostly stuck with his Army buddies and saw Bud away from the beach. I didn't even know he was deployed. It's going to be ugly when he finds out King is with his sister. Shit, I'm sweatin' bullets. This sucks.

Layers of the Soul

Skyla

It's Friday evening, the day after I saw Chase surfing. I only spoke to him on the phone last night because unbeknownst to him, I drove into the nearest town that has some decent shopping spots. I needed to purchase a surprise for him.

I kept thinking he'd tell me on the phone about the surfing, but he didn't, and it was probably because he was too busy trying to convince me to spend the night. I hope he tells me about it soon.

Opening the door with a big grin on his handsome face, he pulls me into his arms like he hasn't seen me in months. He leans back, grabs my face and gives me a passionate kiss as I drop my overnight bag to the floor.

"Guess what today is," he says.

He's adorable when he acts like a teenager.

"I don't know, what?"

"It's the weekend, which means you have to stay the night. You can't tell me no because you agreed, remember?"

"I remember, and I'll be honest, I hated not being in bed with you this week. It felt like the longest week ever. I love you."

He smiles and kisses me again. "I love you, too, and I have a surprise for you."

"No, Chase. No more surprises," I say sternly.

"Baby, you're going to have to get over this. I'm not going to stop doing things for you. I promise this isn't a big one, so come with me." He takes hold of my hand, pulling me behind him.

We go out the glass doors and down to the beach as the sun is setting. I see a blanket and picnic basket with tiki torches lit around it. "Chase, this is romantic."

He runs his hands down my arms and kisses my forehead. "You deserve much more than this, and I'll give you anything, but you're being very difficult about letting me."

"This didn't cost much, right? And it's perfect. See, you don't have to spend a ton of money on me. Being with you near the ocean is all I need."

Chase

Night falls as we eat, talk and make out. We lie on the blanket, and Skyla rests her head on my chest.

"Chase."

"Yes, angel."

"I'm hearing the most comforting sounds."

"What's that?"

"Your heartbeat and the ocean."

"You're so damn special. You never take anything for granted, Skyla. Can I ask what makes you love the ocean so much?"

She leans up on her elbow, so she can see my face.

"The ocean is like infinity. To look out and there be no end in sight is fascinating. When I was a little girl, I'd point out toward the water. 'What's on the other side?' I'd ask my parents.

"I thought if I was a mermaid, then I could go find out," she says, giggling. "It reminds me how gigantic earth is. It's easy to get caught up in our own little world and think our problems are huge, so seeing the ocean is humbling."

"You're right. We're merely a grain of sand in the ocean." I run my fingers through her long hair.

"Exactly," she says with excitement. "It sounds morbid, but I want to be buried in the ocean. All my greatest memories have been near the water, and my body would become part of it, where my soul's been fed the most. I would be giving back what it gave to me, feeding that part of the earth."

I look away from Skyla as tears sting my eyes. I've always had great respect for the ocean, so I wasn't upset that Bud died the way he did, just when he did.

But I'd never thought about it the way Skyla put it. It's comforting to think of his body becoming part of what he loved.

"Chase, are you OK?"

I blink several times, hoping the tears disappear. I haven't cried over Bud since those first few days after he died. I need to tell her, but I can't find the words.

"I'm OK. What you said … it's nice."

She kisses my cheek. "There's another reason I love the ocean, but you'll think I'm a real nerd if I tell you."

"Tell me. I love hearing you speak. You're the most insightful person I've ever met, Skyla."

"Thank you. Since I wrote this for a school paper, I have it memorized, so don't laugh. I swear I'm a big nerd." She chuckles. "OK, let me get serious." She does, and she looks into my eyes with such sincerity.

"I believe the ocean is made up of layers, and they represent each layer of our soul," she says as she lifts my shirt and draws an imaginary line across one of the ripples of my abs.

"The turquoise layer is first. We can see through it and believe we're seeing all that it encompasses, but there's so much more hidden below it. It feels like the safety net of the ocean, but it's only the surface.

"It's the outer layer of our soul. The one we see when we first meet other people or when we don't want to look inside ourselves."

She draws another imaginary line below the first one. "The light blue layer is shallow, and we don't have to think about what lies deeper. We explore it without feeling vulnerable.

"This part of the ocean appears beautiful to the eyes of the beholder because the dark and scary parts lie beneath.

"This is where we look inside ourselves and others a little deeper. We're still comfortable, and the reward outweighs the risk."

Skyla draws another line below the last one. I stare into her sparkling blue eyes, and I'm lost in them as I soak in her words.

"The vast deep blue is the next layer. It's hidden from plain view, and we're often afraid to look into this darker space for fear of what we'll find.

"We feel vulnerable there, yet there are those who get the courage to go deeper to see this extraordinary part of the ocean.

"We want to believe this layer of our soul is who we are. The fears here are scary enough without looking deeper. This is who we let those close to us see, those who we deem worthy, but much more lies underneath."

She leans down and kisses the middle of my stomach before she draws the next line, and if she doesn't stop touching me, she's not going to get to finish her story.

"The last layer is the murky bottom in the farthest depths. When we allow ourselves to move beyond the fear and darkness that reside there, we see all that's good and majestic in this scariest part of the ocean.

"It takes courage to examine this dark and vulnerable layer of our soul. Most people aren't aware that when we embrace our fears, flaws and wrong doings, we find peace and become our best selves. That space becomes a place of strength, resilience and most importantly, forgiveness.

"You did that, Chase. You faced the darkness and your fears, and you found the goodness inside. Now, it's time to forgive yourself."

I grab her and pull her down on top of me. I'm filled with emotions I've never felt before, and all I know to do is to release them on Skyla, so I kiss her, touch her and hug her. I didn't know it was possible to love anyone this much.

She kisses and touches me back, flooding me with her love and affection. Luckily, it's late and no one's around. It's foreplay at its finest once again. The blanket's wadded up and not even under us by the time we're done rolling around.

"I have to get you inside, baby. I think we have sand in every crevice of our body," I say, laughing.

"I think you're right."

"I love you, Skyla. Thank you for giving me a perfect night. You think you don't surprise me, but you do every day. Tonight it's from your insight that I can't get enough of. You're an old soul.

"When I'd watch you play on the beach night after night, I wanted so badly to know what you thought about the sand and the ocean, and you told me. You gave me that gift tonight."

You Read My Mind

Skyla

I have a surprise for Chase, and I think he's going to really like this one. It's not easy, but I convince him to let me shower separately. I hurry, so I have time to fix my hair.

Last night I went shopping for lingerie. I bought a lacy, black bra that has a tiny, baby blue bow in the center.

It came with a black, ruffled garter skirt with satin, baby blue ribbon woven through some of it. It barely goes below my crotch and hooks to black stockings.

The skirt is perfect because you can't tell from the front view that there's nothing underneath. I thought he'd like that part the most.

Thankfully, Chase insists on feeding me all the time, so I had extra money from not buying many groceries.

He knocks on the door, and I can tell he's waiting for me to let him in, but I don't. He tells me he'll be watching TV in his room, and I imagine he's pouting. I find it cute when he does it, which is often when it comes to me.

I'm a nervous wreck as I walk down the hallway. I'm breathing shallow, and my heart feels as if it's trying to escape. He has seen me naked. Why am I so nervous?

Probably because I know I'm going to be on exhibit for several minutes as he enjoys the view. Although, it might cause him to attack me immediately. I quietly giggle when I think about it.

Chase

After foreplay on the beach, I'm ready to bury myself in Skyla, but for some reason, she insists on showering separately, and I don't like it one bit.

I shower and go to find her, but she won't let me in the spare bedroom she's using. I know she has a right to some privacy, but she got me really worked up on the beach.

At least she'll be in my bed tonight. I hated that she wasn't sleeping with me this week. I couldn't convince her to stay over no matter how hard I tried, and I tried hard.

If anyone had told me nine months ago that today I'd be begging a woman to sleep at my house so I can make love to her and snuggle, I'd say they were insane.

Yet here I am, under the thumb of Skyla Moore, and I love every second of it, except for when I don't get my way, which is right now.

I'm in bed watching TV, trying to find something to take my mind off of sex. I'm finally relaxed and not thinking about the dirty things I want to do to Skyla when she walks into my bedroom and throws the biggest match yet on the fire.

She's wearing lingerie.

I'm not talking about the romantic, cute shit, either. She's wearing the X-rated, fill my fantasy kind, and she looks damn good in it. I turn off the TV and throw the remote to the floor as I scan every gorgeous inch of her.

"Oh, baby, I don't know how you did it, but you read my mind. I've dreamed about seeing you in lingerie, and you look even better in it than I pictured. You're hot, Skyla."

Her face turns a little red, and she doesn't move. She looks terrified, and I can see that I'm going to have to go get her. This must be the first time she's done anything like this.

I stalk toward her, never taking my eyes off of her luscious body. I cup her face and give her a deep kiss. When I let go of her lips, she smiles and gazes up at me.

"You like?" she asks.

"Baby, I love."

I run my hands down her arms and up her waist until they're on the sides of her breasts. My thumbs begin circling over her nipples through the racy bra she's wearing.

They harden under my thumbs, and I get even harder, which I didn't think was possible at this point. Her eyes flutter closed as she clenches my waist and tilts her head back.

She's waiting for me to pleasure her, and that makes me crave her even more. I gradually run my nose up her chest to her neck, breathing in her clean, sweet smell before I lick and bite it, taunting her.

Running her nails down my bare back, she lets out an erotic moan.

"Oh sweet, Skyla. You're a fantasy come true," I whisper into her ear. My hands run back down the curves of her body while I probe her mouth with my hot tongue, sweeping it with hers, tasting all of her candy mouth.

I slip my eager fingers up under her skirt to find there's nothing underneath.

Hell. Yes. "You have no panties on, which means you're going to keep this on while I fuck you hard." I growl against her mouth.

She giggles. Why she finds that phrase funny I have no idea. I pull her over to the bed, take off my boxer briefs and get a condom from the nightstand.

She grabs it out of my hand. "Let me," she says before she rips open the package. She strokes me several times before she slides it on, and it takes all my will not to explode.

I scoot back onto the bed. She climbs up into my lap and straddles me, lowering herself onto my rock hard erection. Her arms go around my neck as her head falls back, and I can see on her face that she already feels good.

My hands work their way down the top of her smooth thighs until I reach the stockings. They're so damn sexy.

My fingertips glide along the clips hooked to them, and I don't know what it is about stockings and garter belts, but damn she knew what to wear to drive me crazy.

I hold her waist, moving her up and down on top of me. The friction against her wet, tight flesh is driving my rhythm.

The pleasure I feel on every nerve ending in my body is mind-blowing. Why I ever wanted to numb myself with drugs is beyond me.

It's a hot, burning sensation that feeds my new addiction—Skyla. I crave her, and the more of her I have, the more of her I want.

She begins bouncing harder on top of me until she's arching her back, moaning wildly. It sends more of the fiery burn coursing through my veins.

I pull her down hard onto me until we explode simultaneously. I know this because her muscles are squeezing my cock like a vice, and the pleasure is better than anything I've ever felt in my life.

I pull her against me, burying my face into her neck as I close my eyes and come down from the high her body has sent me on.

After falling back onto the bed, she lies on top of me, straddling me still. My hands are resting on her firm ass, her sultry breath on my neck.

"Damn, girl. You can surprise me anytime you want. You won't hear any complaints from me."

I feel her smile against my neck, and all is perfect in our world. Nothing's going to mess this up.

Happy Birthday

Skyla

I met Bud's friends in mid-October. It's now three days before Christmas, and I can't begin to express how wonderful my relationship is with Chase. Our love grows stronger every day.

We also spend time with Eric and Andy, surfing and hanging out. We enjoyed watching the Vans Triple Crown of Surfing competition together this month, and Chase and I are supposed to spend Christmas day with Eric and his family.

Lee informed me he won't make it home until closer to New Year's, and although I hate for him to spend the holiday in the desert, it gives me more time to tell Chase that I'm Nixie. Eric and I are going to break it to him the day after Christmas.

The longer I know Chase, the more I see what a great human being he is. He has the biggest heart that he hid for far too long. I pray that he'll accept what is and continue to love me regardless of our connection to Bud. I couldn't bear to lose him.

Today is my twenty-first birthday, and the guys insisted they take me out since I'm legal now, but I told them I wanted to spend time with them on the beach.

Chase swears he can go to bars and not drink. Even if he can handle it, he might get moody, and I put moody Chase on permanent vacation a long time ago. I'm not giving him a chance to pay a visit on my birthday.

I wear my pink, strapless sundress and put curls in my long blonde hair. After slipping on some sandals, I walk to Chase's.

He's been begging for two weeks to buy me a damn car. A freakin' car. No way. Now he's telling me he's buying me one when Lee returns from deployment and takes his car back. I agreed so he would drop the issue.

He's always determined to get his way and will act like a child wanting candy in the grocery store if he doesn't get it. He'll ask you over and over again, minus the tantrum. I still find it cute but exhausting.

Chase doesn't answer the door, so I walk around to the back. Right on the beach is a table set up with balloons tied to it. Chase, Eric, Andy, and the couples I met at the bar are hanging out near it. Wow, some females are here.

I hardly know them, so I feel like the charity case birthday girl. I can only imagine how embarrassing I was at the bar that night after how much alcohol I consumed, but it's nice they came.

Eric sees me and points. Chase turns around and practically runs to me, picking me up into a hug.

"Happy Birthday, angel."

"Thank you, but I think that might be the fifth time you've said it today."

"I hope you don't mind that we invited some people to hang out with us."

"I don't mind, but I feel like a charity case."

"Skyla, you are the furthest from that. Please don't feel that way. I've only known one other person as likeable as you. Eric said our friends you met at the bar really liked you."

"Who's as likeable as me?" I bet he's speaking of Bud.

"Um, it's another friend I want to talk to you about soon but not tonight. Tonight is about you." He gives me a kiss. He's ready to tell me about Bud. This is the best birthday gift he could give me.

We walk to the beach where everyone is waiting, and they all wish me happy birthday. Chase even got me a cake. I look at it and become teary eyed.

"Baby, what's wrong?"

"I haven't had a birthday cake since I was like twelve. It's sweet of you to get me one."

"Actually, Eric insisted on getting you the cake. I was a little aggravated at first because he had the bakery put all the colors of your bright bikinis on it. I hit him, so I'm over it now."

"Chase!"

He shrugs his shoulders. "Sorry, I didn't like thinking of him admiring you in your bikinis."

I'm really embarrassed and pray the two of them tell no one else that story. I look at the cake, and there's a surfboard in one corner and a mermaid in the other.

Chase probably told Eric about me wanting to be a mermaid, but I know the real reason Eric did it. I feel a pain in my chest. Nixie. It's as if Bud's channeling through them. Eric comes over to me as I admire the cake.

"Do you like it?"

"This means so much to me, Eric." Since finding out who I am, he seems more drawn to me but not in a romantic way. He treats me like a cousin or sister. I wish my brother was this open with me.

"I love it, Shooter." I manage to grin at him before he grabs me and hugs me tight.

"Happy Birthday, Nixie," he says sweetly in my ear. "Bud would've done this for you. I could never replace him, but I promise to look out for you, whatever you need. It's the least I can do for Bud."

"You're a sweetheart, Eric."

"Hey, break it up over here. Are you moving in on my girl again?" Chase wraps his arms around my waist from behind me.

"No, asshole. I'm giving my new baby sister a hug on her birthday."

Chase gives me a kiss on my neck.

"Oh, well, you can call her your sister all you want."

Eric rolls his eyes as Andy walks up.

"Let her go, Chase, so I can give her a hug on her birthday," Andy says.

"Fine," he says, pouting. "I'm going to get your gift." He kisses my cheek before jogging to the house.

"Happy Birthday, Nixie."

"Thanks, Andy."

"I hear it will be public knowledge in a few days. I hope he can handle this," he says.

"So do I," Eric adds.

I glance at both of them. "I'm not going to give him a choice. I could never accept him leaving me now."

After a few minutes, Chase runs back up to me with a surfboard. It has a big bow on it, and it's top of the line, of course.

"Please don't get mad at me. I figure it's the next best thing to a car."

"Thank you, sweetie. I love it, and I can't wait to use it."

He flashes me a proud smile, and I'm glad I didn't give him grief about buying it. I can tell he really wants to spend his money on me. It's just hard to get used to.

After a while, we go into the house so everyone can drink. Chase doesn't seem fazed by it, giving most of his attention to me. He seldom leaves my side, holding my hand and kissing me occasionally.

I notice that each person stares at us intently several times throughout the night.

"Chase, why does everyone keep staring at us?"

"I think they're surprised to see how we are together ... how I am with you. They've never seen me with a girlfriend, so I think it's shocking them. They'll have to deal with it because I'm not letting you go anywhere." He kisses my forehead.

***

We're finally alone around midnight, so Chase quickly carries me to bed.

"For your birthday, I'm going to make you feel really good by tasting every sweet part of you, but I have another gift for you first."

I bite my tongue. "OK, where is it?" I ask as I scoot up to the head of the bed and wait. "I want it now, so hurry up," I say, teasingly.

He grins and gets a tiny, white box out of his dresser. It's rectangular with a red bow tied around it.

"You have to promise you'll tell me if you're not ready to accept this one."

"OK, I promise to be honest." He hands me the box, and I open it. There's a key! "Chase, I told you not to buy me a damn car." I'm sure he can't miss the frustration in my voice.

"That's not to a car. It's the key to this house. I didn't say mine because I want it to be ours." He sits down on the bed in front of me.

"Skyla, will you move in with me? I can't wake up another morning without you next to me. I want your happy face to be the first thing I see every day."

He's so sweet and sincere. I smile big and jump into his lap. "Yes, yes, yes. I'd love to move in here with you." I give him a big kiss on the cheek and hug his neck.

"Since you'll only stay overnight on the weekends, I thought I'd have to do some convincing."

"I've always wanted to, but I didn't want you to wake up one day and realize I was living here because of how much of my stuff I'd gradually brought over. I wanted you to ask me."

"Baby, I need to spank your ass." He flips me from his lap to the bed on my stomach, and before I can scream, he's swatting my butt.

"Stop, Chase!" I yell while giggling the entire time. After a handful of swats, he finally stops.

"I would've moved your cute ass in here two months ago if I'd known you'd say yes. I didn't ask since you wouldn't even stay through the week. You deserve birthday spankings, too." He begins swatting my butt again. I finally get turned over on my back.

"Angel, you've made me ecstatic tonight. I feel like it's my birthday."

"Now, you need to give my body its birthday present." I give him what I'm guessing is my best alluring look.

"Oh, you're getting it alright."

"This is the best birthday I've ever had. Thank you, Chase. I love you so much."

***

I wake up alone in bed. I will definitely tease him for this since it's the first morning after he asked me to move in. After dressing, I go downstairs and find a note on the table saying that Eric had shown up to surf with him.

I wonder if he's trying to get time in with Chase in case he flips and doesn't want to speak to him. I'm instantly nauseated. I have to make Chase understand why we waited to tell him.

I leave him a note that I'm going home for a while. I'm eager to pack. After I'm home for an hour, there's a knock at the door.

My brother is standing in front of me. *Shit*. I didn't know he was coming home this soon.

"Lee, why didn't you tell me you were coming home early?"

"I wanted to surprise you for your birthday, but you know the military; it got pushed back a day." He drops his stuff in the family room. "I had a friend pick me up."

This is bad. Lee hates Chase. Well, he only knows him as King, but he blames him for Bud's death. I'd planned to break the news gently to Lee when he got here, but I thought I had more time to tell Chase first.

As soon as I get a minute away from Lee, I text Chase, telling him I'll be back over later. I don't want him showing up here. I guess I'm going to be telling Lee first.

"I'll be here for two weeks, so I'll be able to take care of getting us our money. I can't wait until you're back in college. So, who is this guy you're seeing and these other friends you wrote me about?"

I think I'm going to vomit. "Um, they're some surfers I met on the beach. Are you hungry? I'll fix you some lunch."

"That'd be great. I need some good food for a change." He stretches out on my couch and turns on the TV way too loud.

I go into the kitchen and start pulling ingredients out of the fridge and cabinets. I'll feed Lee first and let him nap. Then, when he's appeased, I'll break the news that I'm in love with King.

My Worst Nightmare

Chase

I come in from surfing and see a note from Skyla on the kitchen island. She went home to pack. That's perfect. Her stuff moved to our house is a step closer to her being completely mine.

I decide to go help her after I shower. I miss her already, and it will get her fine ass back here quicker. It's only two days until Christmas, and I really want her out of her house by then.

I park and knock on the door. It opens, and fury rushes through me faster than it ever has in my life.

"Rock, what the fuck are you doing at Skyla's?"

"Excuse me? I could ask you the same fucking thing," he says.

About that time, Skyla slides between him and the door, and I feel like I'm going to go into a blind fit of rage seeing her body touch his.

Rock is Bud's cousin, and we don't like each other– at all. He blamed me for Bud's death, and we didn't get along even before that.

Luckily, I seldom had to look at his face, but why in the hell he's at Skyla's is beyond me. I know in my heart she wouldn't cheat on me.

"Why the hell is King here, Nixie?" Rock asks.

"Lee, calm down," she says, staring at me the entire time.

Skyla is Nixie, and Lee is Rock.

Everything starts to go black. I stumble and then lean over, putting my hands on my knees. This can't be real. *No!* It's a nightmare. Skyla walks up to me and puts her hand on my shoulder.

"Chase, are you OK?"

"Nixie, tell me this is not the guy you've been seeing."

"No, this can't be happening!" I scream at the top of my lungs as I grab my head and pace in her yard.

"Lee, what the hell is wrong with you?" Skyla asks, spinning around to face her brother.

"Nixie, this is the druggy that cost Bud his life."

She turns back around to face me. I stop walking and stare at her, seeing the anguish in her eyes. I imagine the last two months are rushing through her mind the way they are mine.

Everything we didn't piece together but somehow should've. I thought the hell I was living in was over, but it's only beginning.

"Skyla, I'm sorry. I had no idea. I'm leaving, and I'll never hurt you again," I say as I hurry to my car.

"Chase, no. You can't leave!" she yells, running after me.

"Nixie, don't you dare," Rock says.

"Shut up, Lee. He's not who you think he is."

"Yes, he is, and I can't believe you fell for his shit."

She grabs my arm as I try to get into my car.

"Get off of me, Skyla."

"No! You can't walk away from me, from us!" She's crying hysterically. "I don't care what Lee thinks, Chase. I know the real you. I know the good person you are. You promised not to push me away again!"

I manage to get into the car. Skyla's pulling on me to get back out. Her hands locked around my arm feel like a tourniquet, cutting off my blood supply. Each scream from her lungs feel like gravel filling mine, suffocating me.

"Skyla, let me go, now. You're Nixie. I'm no good for you."

She continues to wail, tears pouring from her eyes.

"No, Chase. I love you. You can't do this." She's frantically pulling on my arm the entire time. "Please, please don't leave me! Chase, don't do this to us!"

"I'll never deserve to be with you. Get off of me, now!"

I've never raised my voice to her or denied her anything until now, and it hurts so fucking bad. She lets go of me, screaming as I shut the door. All I want to do is hold her and tell her I love her.

I want to tell her how sorry I am for all the pain I caused her the last year. All the grief she's suffered from losing Bud ... her Bud. The chain reaction my selfish, awful behavior caused.

I should be in front of a firing squad for sleeping with Bud's Nixie. This is purgatory. Why did I believe for a second that I deserved happiness and would get it? I have to get off this fucking island.

I tear into my house and up to my bedroom. Grabbing a suitcase, I throw shit in it, trying to hurry before Skyla shows up. I can't hear her cries again. I'm out the door in minutes, taking off in my Jeep as I call Eric.

"Hey, bro," he says.

"Eric, I need you to handle the deals we have set up. I have to get off this fucking island."

"Bro, wait."

"Just say you'll do it!"

"Fuck, you know."

"What did you say?"

"Chase, I'm sorry."

"You knew who Skyla was and didn't tell me? Did she know, too?"

"Yes, but not at first. Man, listen to me. I found out the night Andy and I took her to the bar. I didn't tell you because you would've fallen apart, and you were finally doing better. I knew you wanted Skyla, and I thought if you two fell in love, you'd be able to survive finding out."

"How could you? How could she?"

"Chase, please try to understand, and don't do anything stupid. Bud wanted you two together. Don't lose the best person that has and will ever be in your life.

"She found out later, and I've kept her from telling you. She wanted to, and I stopped her."

"You're dead to me, Eric," I say and hang up. I've lost everyone.

Skyla

I'm in the kitchen fixing Lee something to eat, and I have the sink water running.

Yelling instantly fills the house, and I hear Chase's voice. I hadn't heard him knock. I run to the door and slide past my brother as my perfect world comes crashing down on me.

Chase looks as if he wants to die when he discovers that Rock is my brother. Lee tells me Chase is responsible for Daniel's death. I've never believed that for one second. Bud was responsible for his own poor choices.

Chase tells me he's leaving me, and I beg him not to. I tell him not to listen to Lee who keeps running his mouth, saying hurtful things about him.

"I don't care what Lee thinks, Chase. I know the real you. I know the good person you are. You promised not to push me away again!" I cry out in agony, but he yells at me and leaves.

I go up to my brother and push him with all the strength I can muster, which is a lot since I'm furious with him.

"Nixie, what the hell is your problem?"

"You're the problem. You may know the old King, but you don't know Chase. You just want someone to blame for Bud's stupid decisions."

"Don't you speak of him that way."

"Don't you disrespect him by treating his best friend and me like shit! Do you even know what Chase has done since Bud died?"

"I don't need to know. He's a spoiled, rich boy strung out on drugs, who obviously didn't squeeze enough out of our family, so he's getting his piece of ass from my sister."

I slap him hard across the face. "Get out of my house. Take your damn car and leave!"

"Nixie, you're so naïve. You've always been too nice and trusting. Go ahead and be with him, but don't call me crying when you see the true person he is." Lee gets his stuff in the house and leaves.

I run until I'm at Chase's, but the Jeep is gone, and I know he is, too. I stand in his driveway and scream. His porch becomes my bed for I don't know how long before I walk back home.

Eric's parked in my driveway. He gets outs and runs to me, pulling me into his arms.

"Skyla, I'm sorry. Chase called me."

I jerk away. "Did he tell you where he's going? You have to help me find him. I have to get him to see that this doesn't change things. If anything, I love him more because I know how much Bud loved him."

"What the hell happened? He wasn't supposed to know yet, and he took it worse than I expected."

"It's because Lee showed up. I didn't get to tell Chase first. I think that's why he took it so hard and freaked out."

"Shit, that's the last person he needed to see when he found out."

I wrap myself in Eric's arms. I know he's hurting and is as scared as I am. "I still think we did the right thing, Eric, so don't feel guilty. We'll get him back."

Eric lets me go. "Chase said I'm dead to him."

"He doesn't mean that. You know he doesn't. How long do you think he'll be gone?"

"I'm sorry, but he's leaving Oahu, and it sounded like he was driving when he called me, so he's probably on his way to the airport."

"Then we have to go get him."

"He'll be gone before we get there. Chase has millions of dollars, Skyla. He can be off this island almost the second his feet touch the airport.

"He can get first class on the first flight leaving. I think I know where he's going, but I'm begging you to wait to go there. He needs time. I know how he is when he's upset and angry, and he won't listen."

"Where's he going?"

"I imagine he'll end up in Maui. He has a home there."

"He hadn't even told me about his house."

"He didn't want you to know. He was going to surprise you with it later. If you haven't noticed, he loves surprising you."

I break down again, so Eric walks me into my house with his arms around me.

"I don't have the money to go there right now, but I'll have it this week. I'm getting some money, and it's quite a bit."

"Skyla, I'll pay your flight if it comes down to it, but I don't want you going there now. You have to give him time. Maybe he'll come back on his own."

"I don't know how I'll wait," I say.

"We have to have faith it'll work out. I always knew Chase was a good person. Even when he was making all the wrong choices, he was there for the rest of his friends and me, but since he got clean ... I see the great man that he is.

"I'm praying us telling him that repeatedly will sink into his thick skull. Skyla, I've never known anyone who loves someone the way he loves you. He worships you."

"If you're right, then I'll get through to him. He gave me a key to his place last night. He wrapped it in a box and gave it to me as a birthday gift. He asked me to move in with him." I smile from the sweet memory.

"Wow, King let a chick move in his bachelor pad," Eric says, leaning over and bumping my shoulder with his while we sit on my couch.

"I'm going to stay there in case he comes back."

"I think that's a good idea, but it might take a while."

"Christmas is in two days, Eric."

"I know, and I'm sorry. I guess we shouldn't have chanced waiting this long to tell him. Unfortunately, I don't think that'll make him come back sooner."

He offers me a ride to Chase's since I need to take several belongings, so I pack some bags and go. I convinced Chase to be with me before, so I'll do it again.

Self-Destruction

Chase

I really need a fucking jet. After booking the next flight to Maui, I wait anxiously to board the plane. I should probably go to the mainland, but I didn't have enough time to prepare for that. I'm not going to be able to leave work and my house that long.

If I know Skyla like I think I do, she'll be waiting for my return. Figures the sweet angel still thinks I'm a saint. I can't believe she's not pissed at me.

Give it time. She'll come to realize the pain I caused her, and if her brother gets in her head, then she'll definitely start hating me.

***

I get to Maui and rent a car. I can't get to my place fast enough. I have so much rage inside me, and I know exactly what I'm going to do when I get there. I walk in and waste no time.

First it's the lamp on the end table. I throw it across the room, shattering the glass into hundreds of pieces. Then it's every plate and glass in the kitchen. I throw a chair and break every picture.

"Fuck!" I scream, over and over. I throw or break every item in my house other than the couch and bed until there's nothing left to destroy.

It was wrong to waste perfectly good stuff, but if I don't, I'm going to do something I'll really regret, something I swore I'd never do again.

Every time I let myself feel the stabbing pain of losing Skyla, I scream at the top of my lungs. This goes on for hours until my throat burns, and it reminds me of the feel of whiskey sliding down it.

I won't drink. My life is fucked up enough. A gateway drug ... a gateway straight to hell.

Surprisingly, the police never show from the screaming. I have to wear my shoes from all the glass on the floor. I guess the bright side is that I'll have plenty to clean up tomorrow to keep me busy.

I find my bed and crash on it, praying that somehow tomorrow will be better, but I already know it won't. Life will never be better without Skyla in it.

Christmas Blues

Skyla

My cell phone rings, and I see that it's Lee. He's tried to reach me for two days, but I never answered. It's Christmas day, and I'm beginning to feel guilty since he doesn't know I'm staying at Chase's.

If he's been stopping by my house, then he's probably worrying about me, so I answer.

"Nixie, we need to talk. Where are you?"

"I'm at King's."

"Unbelievable."

"He's not here. He left the island after you made him feel so much guilt."

"I don't feel sorry for him, sis. Were you even planning on seeing me today? It's Christmas. Does the asshole still live in that fat house by the beach where Bud died?

"You're the asshole."

"Nixie, are you going to stay mad at me?"

"As long as you keep talking bad about him. If you want to speak to me further, then you're going to be respectful to me."

He's quiet. "OK, fine. Is that still where he lives?"

"Yes."

"I'll be there soon."

"Wait, Lee. I already purchased a lot of groceries for today, so why don't I gather them up, and we'll go to my house. I'll at least cook you dinner today."

"That would be nice, sis. I'll be there shortly."

I pack up groceries and wait on the steps for Lee. I'm not about to let him in Chase's home. I already told Eric I'm not coming to dinner. He was upset with me, but I knew I needed to see my brother.

I leave Chase a note in case he comes home. I don't want to leave his bed, but I can't desert my brother on Christmas Day, no matter how mad I am at him.

We get to my place, and I start removing food from the bags. Lee's studying me as he leans against the kitchen counter. I feel his eyes on me no matter where I move.

"Why are you at his place if he's not on the island?"

"He asked me to move in with him on my birthday. I have a key."

"Dammit, Nixie, please don't."

"Lee, I love him. I've loved him almost since I met him. He might've saved my life, too. Some guys stopped me on the beach one night and told me that I couldn't leave. King ran them off. I really believe they were going to hurt me.

"He'd been watching me walk on the beach for months because he worried about me being out there late at night, and he didn't even know who I was."

"Why the hell were you out there, Nixie?"

"I feel closer to Bud when I'm near that spot. King went to rehab right after Bud died and has changed. If you only knew how well he treats me.

"No one has ever loved me as much as he does. I can't be without him, and I'm determined to get him back."

"I can't accept that. You deserve better. You two really had no idea about your connection with Bud?"

"I figured it out a few weeks after we met, but I didn't tell him for this very reason. I was going to tell him tomorrow, but you came home early.

"Since Bud gave us all nicknames, they didn't know me by Skyla or you as Lee. I didn't know them by their real names, either. I only made the discovery because I found a picture of Bud in King's house.

"Don't you see how this was meant to be? We were all brought together without even knowing. Bud's friends have really been there for me. I don't understand why you think they're evil."

"Bud would never want this."

"You're wrong. Let's drop this. I want to spend time with you, and then I want to get back to his house in case he comes home."

After dinner, Lee drops me off at Chase's, and I can tell he hates it. He'll have to get over it. I go inside and see that Chase is still gone, so I call Brooke in California.

"Merry Christmas, Nixie. How are you?"

"Not good, and it's too much to tell over the phone. I really need you right now. Could you come here right away if I pay your ticket?"

"It's Christmas Day."

"I know. I meant in a couple of days. I really need you."

"Yes, but I can't let you pay my way, and I don't have the money. I don't feel right asking Rob since he pays for so much already."

"Please, Brooke. Let me buy your ticket. I miss you, and I need my girlfriend."

"Rob's going to freak out, but I still have a couple of weeks before school starts, so I guess I could."

"Thank you so much. I get my trust money tomorrow, so I'll purchase your ticket then."

"OK, girl. Get it set up."

***

Chase has been gone for three days. I'm definitely depressed. I quit my job for him weeks ago, and I don't start school for two more weeks, so I have all day and night to miss him and worry.

I've stopped leaving him messages. All I do is lie in his bed and cry. I hear a knock on the door, and it's Lee.

"Sis, I have your check, and don't you want to spend more time with me before I leave?"

"Can you take me to the bank? Also, can you take me to the airport tomorrow to pick up Brooke?"

"Why is Honey coming here?"

"To be here for me. I don't think you're grasping how serious of a situation this is. It's my life we're talking about, and I plan to spend the rest of it with Chase. I love him and miss him. Brooke's coming here to support me."

"OK, fine, but you need to sign these papers for the trust. Don't blow this money, Nixie. It's your future."

"Really, Lee? I've always been careful with my money since I've never had much of it. I am buying Honey's ticket though since she can't afford it. That's worth every penny. Let me get my shoes, and we'll go to the bank."

Lee doesn't get it. He hasn't loved anyone the way I love Chase or King. Who the hell knows what we're supposed to call each other now?

I always called Lee "Rock" until Bud died, and he's always called me "Nixie." But like for Chase and his friends, it's been too hard for me to call Lee and Brooke by their nicknames. Bud named Brooke "Honey."

Lee has no issue with calling us by our nicknames, so I guess it's time I get back to doing the same.

Chase

I need the pain to go away. The emptiness I feel is gut-wrenching. I need Skyla just to breathe.

I've barely eaten in days, and I only know what day it is because I can't forget the amount of time I've been away from her. I need to touch her skin, see her smile and feel the joy that radiates from her.

I can't believe I spent Christmas alone in this bed. It was going to be a special day spent with my friends and her. At least she had Rock to spend the time with.

It's pathetic how I cry over her all day. She was leaving me voicemails until yesterday. It pains me to hear them, but I listen to hear her voice. She still wants me. After everything, she still wants to be with my sorry ass.

The pain I'm putting her through makes me sick, but the pain I caused her from Bud's death is unforgivable. The thought of it cuts through my core. It feels like a knife chopping me into pieces. She has to get over me.

Last Ditch Effort

Eric

I don't know what to do to help my friends. Skyla's not even the same person. There's no life left in her, and I can't even imagine what King's going through. If he doesn't come back soon, I'm going to have to go looking for him.

My phone rings, and I see that it's Skyla.

"Hi, girl. Are you doing OK?" I ask gently.

"No, I miss him, Eric. The pain is unbearable."

"I wish I could do something to help."

"I have to go find him. I'm only giving it a couple more days," she says.

"I'm going with you."

"My friend, Brooke, will be here later today. She can go with me."

"You don't even know where you're going. I have to go with you. I know where he lives and how the flights work. You're too upset to deal with it on your own."

"Fine."

"How are things with Rock?"

"He's an ass, but he's taking me to pick up Brooke. I told him he better not mention Chase."

I've really had it with Rock treating her like shit.

"Call me tomorrow, and we'll work out the arrangements to go to Maui," I say.

We hang up, and I decide that tonight I'm finding Rock.

***

It's nine at night, so I figure Rock's had plenty of time to pick up Skyla's friend and drop them off. He'll probably be at the bar I know he frequents since he'll be pissed and upset over Bud. He's not the only one that's had this shit thrown back in his face.

I pull into the bar parking lot and see his car. It's the one Skyla's been driving. He's sitting on a bar stool inside and looks up at me when I pull out the one next to him.

"Shooter," Rock says before he takes a drink of his beer.

"Rock."

"I guess it wasn't enough I had to see King's ugly face."

"We need to talk. I can't sit back and watch you hurt Skyla."

Rock looks at me with anger in his eyes.

"Don't tell me how to treat my baby sister. Just great, I guess you're the other one she's close to."

"Rock, you really have no fucking clue how things were before Bud died or since. You need to hear some things, or you're going to lose your sister, too.

"Besides how damn sweet Skyla is, the thing I love about her the most is the happiness and positive attitude that oozes from her. It's gone, and I don't think it'll come back if she doesn't get to be with King."

"I can't forgive him for what he did to Bud."

"I don't know what gave you the idea that King was the bad influence. It was Bud who got King hooked on hard drugs. I saw how it all went down, and it tore me apart.

"I loved Bud, but he wasn't perfect like you want to believe. He wanted someone to do coke with him, and I think he wanted it to be King because he had an unlimited supply of cash to get the shit for them. He also had the house to bring the women to.

"I know Bud cared about King, but he destroyed his life. It wasn't the other way around like everyone outside of our circle wants to think. I wouldn't lie to you, man."

"But King supplied him time after time."

"Yes, but only after Bud got him hooked. On top of what happened before Bud died, for nine months after, King punished himself.

"He did go right to rehab, which was good, but then he shut himself up in his house. He didn't do shit. He didn't spend one minute with a woman. He never touched his board. He did nothing.

"Then your angel of a sister walked into our lives, and we all came to life again. It was like Bud put her there to make it happen.

"We love her, man. We'd never hurt her, and King wants to give her everything. He adores her, and you'd see that if you'd get past your fucking anger."

I'm shocked he listened to all of that. Probably because he doesn't know what the hell to do for Skyla any more than I do. This right here was my last idea. Rock takes another swig of his beer and looks at me.

"Bud struggled with alcohol and drugs before he ever got to Oahu, but it wasn't bad. I assumed because King had money that he got Bud to try the harder shit."

"I don't believe Bud intended to take advantage of King, but he did, and he did it for a long time. It was the perfect set up for Bud because King won't let his friends pay for a damn thing.

"Bud was a good person. He had that happy energy that Skyla exudes, but his mind wasn't healthy like hers. He was self-destructive, and he about took King down with him. I swear it's the truth."

"Did Nixie send you down here?"

"No, she doesn't know. I did this because I care about her and King. If they don't get back together, then I believe King will slowly die, and she'll go back to California. We all lose her then, including you."

Rock drops his head and grasps the top of his beer bottle, twirling it around on the bar. "She's really pissed at me."

"I know she's all you have left, and if you want her to be on this fucking island when you get back from deployment, then you need to forgive King and let him love her.

"He'll take better care of her than any other man could. It's pathetic how much he worships her. He treats her like his queen."

"So, where is he if he loves my sister so damn much?"

"He's punishing himself again. He still blames himself for Bud dying, so I imagine he feels responsible for all of her grief. You might be the only one who can change that."

"I've never liked King. He always acted like an arrogant ass. I can't bow down to him or apologize."

"I'm not asking you to. Just tell him you know it's not his fault Bud died. Then let him be with Nixie without giving them shit over it.

"Whether you want to believe it or not, Bud wanted the two of them together. He planned on fixing them up when she got here. He talked about it all the time.

"Ultimately, Bud made his own choices. He chose to surf that night when he was fucked up. It's not King's fault, and he's punished himself enough over it. If you don't want to do it for him, do it for Skyla."

Rock doesn't say anything. I sit quiet, knowing he's trying to come to terms with the fact that Bud was flawed. None of us want to admit it, but it has to be acknowledged to move forward.

"Alright. I'll do this for Nixie and Bud but not for King. He still played a role in my cousin's drug use, and I don't know if I can get past that.

"I'll admit, I know Bud wanted them together, and I can tell my sister loves King. It's killing me to see her hurting like she is. Where is the fucker?"

"He has a house in Maui. Skyla's going there with me in two days."

"You want me to fly to Maui to tell him this shit?" he asks, sounding surprised.

"King needs an intervention, and he needs each of us to talk to him if we're going to get him back with Skyla."

"Shit, I can't believe I'm doing this. It's only to make things right with Nixie. She's never been angry at me before, and I hate it."

"Just say you'll do it."

He lets out a deep breath. "Have Nixie get hold of me, and I'll go."

"Thanks, man." He must've already been questioning his behavior. That was way too easy. I figured I'd be leaving here with blood on me, most likely my own.

Skyla

"This is his home?" Brooke asks, sounding shocked as she sets down her suitcase.

"Yep, this is it."

"He has to have millions, Nixie."

"That's what I hear, but you know I don't care."

"I know, but it's so damn cool. Now that your brother's gone, you need to tell me everything. I'm gathering Chase found out the truth."

"Lee came home early, and Chase showed up before I got to tell him that I'm Nixie. He couldn't have found out in a worse way."

I continue to tell Brooke everything. We've been friends since grade school, and we're so much alike that it's weird at times. The only significant difference is our looks and the fact that her self-esteem has went down the toilet since she started dating her loser boyfriend.

She has the prettiest long hair that's between the colors of caramel and honey. Her eyes are brown and have the prettiest speckles of gold in them, another reason Bud called her Honey. He would tease her and tell her that he bet she tasted like honey, too.

He always had a crush on her, but with him leaving California at eighteen, they never had a chance to date. He was too old for her before that.

Brooke and I spend the rest of the day lounging on the beach. I keep my shades on and cry a lot of the time. She holds my hand between the chairs and allows me to be sad.

It's the great thing about girlfriends. They know everything can't be fixed at that moment, and you sometimes need to cry. Chase, Eric and Andy think if I cry, then they need to fix it and fast, joyful tears or not. Men hate to see women cry, but sometimes we have to.

My phone rings, and I frantically grab it out of my swim bag with the hope that it's Chase, but it's Eric.

"Hi, Eric."

"Hi, I have some news. I was going to come by, but I have to get up early and get a lot of work finished since we're going to be gone for a couple of days. Anyway, I talked to your brother."

"You did what?" I ask in total shock.

"I went to see Rock. Don't worry; it went good. I couldn't watch him hurt you and Chase like this, so I had to get through to him. King can't move forward with you if Rock's always there telling him it's his fault."

"Well ... what did he say?"

"Skyla, I hadn't told you because I didn't want to talk bad about Bud, but your brother had to know to forgive King, so you have to know, too. Bud got Chase doing drugs. It wasn't the other way around."

"I already knew that."

"How?"

"Bud told me."

"Why would he admit that?"

"He felt guilty. He thought when I got here, I'd somehow get them to change. I think it's another reason he wanted me with Chase."

"Rock's going to Maui with us, and he's going to tell King that he doesn't blame him, and he's going to tell him to be with you."

I start sobbing, and Eric freaks out, of course. "Skyla, why are you crying? Please stop. I can't stand it."

"I'm sorry, Eric," I say between sniffles. "I can't believe you did that for us. You're the greatest friend."

"I don't want to lose you both. I told you I was going to step in for Bud and be there for you, especially when Chase can't. I meant it. I'll call you tomorrow," he says solemnly.

"I love you, Eric, and Chase will forgive you."

"I love you, too, Nixie."

I end the call and feel hope for the first time in days. I look over at Brooke.

"Eric is someone you need in your life. He's the kind of friend everyone needs in their life."

Finding Chase

Eric

I can't believe we're really going on a hunt for King today. Skyla said she, Rock and her friend will meet me at the airport. She thought it best we leave two cars there in case someone has to come back before everyone else.

I can't believe I caused myself to have to travel with her ass of a brother. King better never pull this kind of shit again.

Skyla comes running toward me as I sit at the gate. I stand before she gives me a huge hug, and I know it's for getting Rock to come along.

Damn, this must be Brooke.

She's gorgeous. She's heaven. She has to sit next to me on the plane.

"Brooke, this is Eric, my friend I was telling you about."

Brooke reaches her hand out to me, and it's soft. Her eyes meet mine, and they sparkle with flecks that look like gold. She's one hot chick, and dammit, if I remember correctly, Skyla said she's taken.

"Hi, Brooke." I flash her a smile.

"Hi, it's nice to meet you, Eric. Skyla has only great things to say about you."

"I'm surprised considering how we first met." I wink at Skyla.

"Shut up, Eric. Do you honestly want me to tell her why I fell into the bathtub?"

"Not yet. Brooke needs to get to know me better first, so she won't think I'm a pig when she hears it."

Yes, I'm trying to flirt. I glance at Rock, and he rolls his eyes.

"Hi, Rock."

"Shooter," he says before he sits down. He leaves two seats between us, and I hope Brooke sits next to me, but Skyla does instead. I see that Brooke is saying something to Rock, so I lean over and whisper into Skyla's ear.

"You need to let her sit by me on the plane, sister."

Skyla laughs. "OK, but don't get your hopes up. I'd like nothing more than to see it happen, but I don't think it can in the few days she's here."

"Move her ass to the island."

"I keep trying," she says quietly while giggling.

Brooke sits by me on the plane, and I gather that she's nervous from the way she fidgets with her delicate hands. "Do you dislike flying?" I ask her.

"No, I don't mind it," she replies.

Awesome. That means I might be making her nervous instead of the fear of crashing into the ocean.

"I know this is awkward. It's great that you came to be here for Skyla. I can already tell that you're sweet like her."

She turns her head to the side and looks up at me. Our faces are not far apart, so I get to see how beautiful she is.

"Thanks. That's nice of you to say. It's weird to hear you call her Skyla. Everyone we both know calls her Nixie. Maybe she doesn't want new people she meets calling her that because it reminds her of Bud."

"Honestly, I don't know what I'm supposed to call her now. I call her Nixie, too. I'd like to call her sis, but I imagine Rock wouldn't appreciate it."

"You two are close, huh?" she asks.

"I think it's safe to say that. She already feels like a sister." I need to shut up. My lack of filter is surely going to get me in trouble if I keep talking.

Now, I feel bad because she's fidgeting with her hands even more. This damn trip is going to be stressful.

Skyla

We land in Maui and get a vehicle. After all that's happened, it's strange for us to be in a car together. It doesn't bother me since I'm with three of the four people I'm closest to, but I know it's uncomfortable for them.

We get to the hotel, and the guys come to my room, so we can get a game plan. They each have their own room, and Brooke and I are sharing one. I glance at Eric and Lee. "I'm going over there first."

"No, Skyla. I don't know what you could walk into," Eric says.

"I agree with Shooter. We need to go first," Lee adds.

"I miss him. It's killing me, and knowing he might be this close to me makes it worse."

"Nixie, I don't think King would do it, but he did have a drug problem, and if he's doing that to numb himself, then you don't need to see him like that," Lee says.

I quickly shake my head. "He won't do it. I know he won't go back to that."

My brother gives me his protective look.

"Sis, let us go first."

"Fine, but plead with him to see me."

Eric walks up and takes hold of my shoulders before he kisses my forehead. "I will. We'll be back and hopefully with him."

They leave, and I pace the room, chewing on my nails.

"Nixie Moore, why didn't you tell me how hot Eric is?"

"I told you he's cute."

"He's far beyond cute."

"You're taken, remember?"

"Yeah, but I'm not blind, and is he always that sweet?"

"Yes, and you deserve someone like that. Rob's an asshole."

"He just has issues."

"Yeah, that he takes out on you, Honey. I wish you would leave him. How many times has he already text you today?"

"A lot, but he worries about me."

"He threw the biggest fit over you coming here. He's controlling."

"That's only because I'll be gone New Year's. I came didn't I?"

"True, and I'm grateful. I can't take this. I'm going to go insane waiting."

"I'm sorry, Nixie. Let's watch a movie to take your mind off of it."

Honey turns on the television, and I pretend to watch as a million images run through my mind. I'm worried Chase and Lee will fight, and this will backfire. I clutch my phone and wait ... and wait ... and wait.

Self-Loathing

Chase

I haven't cleaned up the mess. I don't have the energy. I decide I'll pay people to do it when I leave and make it worth their while. Looking at the glass and broken furniture everywhere makes me feel more punished.

It's a fucked up mess like my life. Last night I used the wall as target practice for the steak knives I repeatedly threw. They're still stuck there like they are in my heart.

The doorbell rings. This can't be good. Only Eric and Andy would suspect I'm here. I open the door, and sure enough, it's Eric but also Rock. Why in the hell is he here? "I made it clear how I feel, Eric," I say before I try to shut the door. Rock grabs it.

"You're letting me in to speak to you. I didn't take one of my days away from that hellhole desert to fly here and have a door shut in my face." Rock looks pissed.

I open it up and move for them to come in. I see the stunned expression on their faces and hear the floor crunch from the glass underneath their feet.

"I see you've been getting some of your anger out," Eric says.

"It's better than the alternative."

"You're right," he says.

They pick up a couple of kitchen chairs from the floor. Rock faces his backward and sits down, leaning on his arms over the top of it. I lean against the counter with my arms crossed and stare at them.

"You need to come back home. You're killing Skyla, leaving her the way you did. You know how much she loves you, and your connection to Bud isn't going to change that. She said it makes her love you more," Eric says.

Picturing her in pain hurts so fucking bad.

"I don't see how she could feel that way. She should be upset with me for all the grief she's had to endure. Why the fuck did she keep something like this from me?"

"We were going to tell you the day after Christmas, but Rock showed up earlier than she expected. She was waiting to tell you until she was sure you loved her enough not to walk away.

"Don't be pissed at her because obviously she had grounds for feeling that way. You did exactly what we feared."

"Don't even say I don't love her."

"I'm not saying you don't love her, but if you love her as much as you always say you do, then you won't leave her. Bud made the choice on his own to surf at night when he was strung out on drugs.

"You fixed what you were doing wrong. You made things more than right because along with getting clean, you treat Skyla like a fucking queen. It's exactly how Bud wanted it. I told Rock everything."

I glance to Rock. I can't imagine why he wants to talk to me, and I really don't want to hear whatever it is he has to say. My heart slams against my chest repeatedly, and I want something else to break.

"King, Eric told me about Bud getting you to try the coke. I know he had an unlimited supply because of you, and that pisses me off, but I'm sure he took advantage of the fact you had money.

"He was responsible for his own actions. Even messed up, Bud knew better than to be out in the water that night. If you were still using and treating Nixie like shit, then I'd say to stay the hell away from her, but it sounds like you've changed.

"You went to rehab and punished yourself for months. I don't know if I'll ever like you, but I hear you treat Nixie well, so you need to go home and take care of her. However, if you ever start the drugs again, I'll make sure she leaves your ass."

I stare at Rock. I don't know if I could ever like him, either, but I'm surprised at what I'm hearing.

"I don't know how to look at her and not think about how upset she's been all these months over Bud. I watched her on the beach for three months before I ever met her, and I saw her pain, not having a clue that it was because she lost him ... that it was because of me."

"Didn't we just cover this?" Rock asks. "You can give Nixie the life she deserves, not the shitty one she was dealt so far. I saw the pain you were in and the way you looked at her when you found out she was Nixie. I can tell you love her.

"I can't stand how depressed she is, so go back to her, and I'll never breathe another word about you being responsible for Bud's death.

"Also, she pushed me and slapped the shit out of me over what I said about you that day, so make things right. I can't stand having her pissed at me," he adds.

I never in my wildest dreams would've thought I'd be hearing this. He hated me, and now he's practically begging me to be with Skyla. Eric made this happen.

"I know how close Bud was to her. He talked about it constantly. I don't deserve to love his Nixie after feeding his addiction."

Eric stands up and launches his chair across the room before getting in my face. "I've fucking had it with you and this self-loathing shit. You don't see it, but it's hurting everyone around you.

"I took it and dealt with what it did to you, me, Andy and our other friends, but I won't stand by and watch you hurt Skyla this way!

"If you feel a need to redeem yourself the rest of your damn life, then do it by taking care of her. You're abandoning Skyla after you told her you'd always be there for her.

"Bud would kick your ass for treating his Nixie this way, and you know it. She's depressed and barely eating. You fucked up everyone's holiday, and she's lain in *your* bed all day every day, clutching her phone, waiting for you to come back to her.

"Yes, you heard that right, *your* bed. That's an actual reason you should be feeling like shit, not all this other nonsense you want to believe. You are your own worst enemy, King."

I've never seen Eric this angry. He smacks my chest with a manila envelope. "Take this. I don't know what it is, but Skyla said it was important for you to see. She's here waiting at the Hyatt Regency Resort, room 522. She wants us to bring you back, but I refuse.

"I only want you to go to her if you're done feeling sorry for yourself and have no intentions of walking out on her again. She doesn't deserve any of this, and I want to know there won't be a repeat.

"You need a fucking shower, too, and seeing this place would scare the shit out of her, so I'm not letting her come here, either. We'll be at the hotel until morning."

Rock points at me. "Don't keep her waiting, King. If she has to come looking for you, then I'll be ahead of her to kick your ass," he says before they both go out the door.

I let out the deep breath I took when I heard she's in Maui. She's so close to me, and thinking about touching her warms me all over.

I'm terrified she's going to see me different once she spends time with me. She'll see me as King, Bud's friend, the drug user and womanizer. Holding the large manila envelope, I fall back on the bed and stare at it. As I run my hand around it, I feel a lot of papers.

I don't know why, but I'm afraid to look inside. Maybe she wrote me a letter. I should've known she was staying at my place ... our place.

Thinking of her waiting in my bed for me day after day crushes me. I left her while she clung to me, begging me not to go. I didn't even let her tell me how she felt, yet she's here still trying to get me back.

Eric's right. I should only go to her if I'm going to stop this shit. I can't hurt her again. I wish Bud was here to tell me it's definitely what he'd want.

Skyla

Jumping off the bed, I run to answer the door. It's Eric and Lee. I move so they can come in before I look behind them, but there's no Chase.

"What happened?" I ask desperately.

"He's here, and he's OK. Well, I wouldn't say he's OK, but he's not using. He's punishing himself with guilt instead," Eric says.

"So, he won't come back to me?"

"We don't know. After yelling at him, I gave him the envelope and told him your room number. I probably could've convinced him to come, but I'm over his shit."

"Why didn't you?" I ask with frustration.

"I want him to be sure, Skyla. You don't deserve this pain. Only he can stop what he's doing to himself."

"Lee, what did you say?"

"Don't worry. I was nice. He's definitely punished himself long enough. He's not the spoiled, arrogant guy I met when I moved here. He's changed. I saw how much he loves you and Bud."

"I'm going over there," I say.

"No, I told him I wasn't letting you. I know you're desperate to get him back, but you deserve someone who's not going to be self-destructive.

"He has to believe he deserves you and believe that this is what Bud would want. He has to make a choice. I think he'll make the right one," Eric says.

I shake my head. "No, give me the address."

Lee walks over and hugs me. My brother rarely does this, so it feels weird to be in his arms. He pulls back but doesn't let me go.

"Sis, you don't need to see his house. He's destroyed it, and he's a mess. People can hurt themselves in more ways than doing drugs. He has to choose to be the strong man you need.

"Don't start a life of enabling him. I know you think you have enough love for the both of you, but if he doesn't think he deserves it, then he'll do this again. If it's not over this, then it will be over something else."

"You're probably right. As painful as it is, I have to wait. We can't fix others. I thought I could fix Chase, but he showed me I can't." I hear Brooke and Eric leave the room. They know Lee and I need to be alone to have this conversation.

He pulls me back against his chest. "Dad ran from his grief over Mom. His job over in that hellhole was his way of self-destructing because he thought it was all he deserved since Mom died and not him.

"I'm sorry, Nixie. I see now that I did the same thing to you, joining the Army and going over there like Dad.

We both walked away from you because we didn't want to deal with our grief. We left you alone.

"You deserve a love you can always count on, one you don't have to chase after. Make King come to you. I can't leave the military right now, but I will try hard to be the brother you deserve, especially when I get back. I love you, sis."

Tears come, stinging before they trickle down my cheeks. "I love you, too, Rock. I love you so much."

He leans back to look at me and smiles.

"You called me Rock again."

"That's who you are. It's time to celebrate Bud's life. I need to continue being the strong woman I grew into. Chase has to choose to live life with me. He's choosing all of this.

"I believe with all my heart that Bud had a hand in bringing all of us together, but we have free will. Now, it's up to Chase to hang on to what Bud gave us."

"You're special, Nixie. You're wise and kind. You always have been. I don't believe King will be able to stay away from you."

Brooke is Heaven

Eric

Brooke and I leave Skyla and Rock alone in her room. It's obvious they're way overdue to have a talk. One of those talks people try their hardest to avoid, especially with family.

Rock's not the man I thought he was. People you hardly know usually aren't. He's better.

We stand in the hallway. Brooke is on one side of the door sitting down on the floor with her legs crossed. I lean against the wall on the other side. We stay like this for several minutes before I hear her crying.

What is this? Everyone's rite of passage?

"Brooke, are you OK?"

Why do we ask this? It's a dumb question to ask people when it's obvious they're upset, but we do it anyway. I guess to break the ice, to say "you can tell me what's wrong even though this is awkward as hell."

"I'm fine," she says between sniffles.

And that's the usual answer people give.

"You don't seem fine."

That really did it. Shit. Now, the girl is sobbing. I know she has a boyfriend, but he isn't here, and I'm not going to let her sit here and cry.

I go sit on the floor next to her and pick up her hand, holding it in mine. She pulls her knees up and lays her head against them.

I shouldn't be thinking about it right now, but her legs are awesome. They're toned and smooth. I'm a guy, so I'm using that excuse.

She keeps sobbing, and I can see that she needs a tissue. This sucks. I can't let her do this in the hotel hallway. I let her hand go and stand up in front of her, reaching my arms out.

"Come on, Brooke. Get up. You're coming with me." She looks up, her face red and swollen, and she's still beautiful. "Come on."

She reaches out and takes my hands, so I can pull her up. She follows behind me down the hall. I pull the room key out of my back pocket and open the door. I step back for her to go in, and she stops. If she's a decent girlfriend, then I expect as much.

"I shouldn't be in your room. I guess you don't know, but I have a boyfriend."

"You need something to blow your nose with, so get in here. I'm going to be your friend."

She walks in, and I follow her inside. I get some tissues in the bathroom and hand them to her. After she dries her face and blows her nose, she leans forward and rests her head against my chest.

I don't know what to do, but it seems she expects me to wrap my arms around her, so I do. It's probably not the best idea, and I can't say I'm only doing it for her, but she genuinely needs it. We both do. This trip sucks.

Brooke smells and feels amazing as I hold her. After a few minutes, she pulls back a little, so I assume she wants me to let her go, but instead, she wraps her arms around my neck and continues to rest her head on my chest.

She fits in my arms perfectly and is petite like Skyla. She looks to be around 5' 5," so I'm guessing I'm about eight inches taller than Brooke.

She's too sweet for words but seems a little broken. I can already tell she's not a cheater, so she must date a loser to be desperate for this kind of hug.

After a few more minutes, I let her go. If I don't, then I'm going to do something I'll regret. I want more than anything to kiss her, so I go sit in a chair in the corner of the room.

She sits on one of the beds and falls back onto it. Damn, her body stretched out looks enticing. It's calling for me to be on top of it.

OK, maybe not, but *my* body is calling to be on top of it. Her sweet smell still lingers on me, and god, I'm drawn to this woman.

"What's got you this upset?"

"I realized from all the stuff you and Rock said that I have some problems in my relationship with Rob. He doesn't treat me good."

I don't want her hurting, but that's the best news I've heard all day, that is if she leaves the asshole.

"Also, I've been there with Nixie through all of her losses. If King doesn't come through, it's going to break her. How long can she be strong? She'll only have Rock and me again."

"And Andy and me. We really care about her and are not going anywhere. I never thought I'd want to get married or have a family, but after caring for Skyla so quickly, I realize I might be boyfriend material after all.

"After seeing how King and Nixie are together, I know I want that. He loves her in a way I've never witnessed before, so he'll come through.

"He just needed to hear from someone on the outside that Bud dying wasn't his fault and that he deserves to be with her. Rock gave him that. He even told him to take care of Nixie. King will show up."

"I think you'll make a great boyfriend. You're so much nicer and more open than any guy I've ever met."

Wow, she said "any." "Thanks. I don't know what your boyfriend does that's wrong, but you at least deserve to be treated with respect."

"He loves me, but he's controlling and doesn't make me feel the greatest about myself."

"Then he doesn't love you the way you deserve, Brooke. I can see you're special."

I watch her swallow hard as she stares at the ceiling. I need to shut up. "I'm sorry. I tend to call things like I see it, and I can be a little too honest at times."

"That's a good thing. It's just not what I want to hear since I love him."

Ouch. Brooke sits up in the bed.

"Shit, I just realized something. I thought Nixie would be going to King's place if they worked things out. If he shows up to the room, I can't be there, so I guess I need to get my own."

"Yeah, that's a definite."

Brooke goes to get her a room, and I rest on the bed. I need to leave her the hell alone. I feel something for her, and I just met her. I don't even know anything about her other than she's sweet, adorable and smells good enough to eat.

I shouldn't expect any less since she's Skyla's best friend. There's a knock at my door, and it's Brooke. She looks upset again.

"What's wrong?"

"They don't have any more rooms."

"Oh, well, I'll see if Rock will let me stay in his. We're getting along better. Maybe he won't care."

"OK, thanks."

I go to Rock's room.

"Sorry, but after today, I want a chick in my bed. I'm going out, and I'm bringing one back here."

"Fine. Good luck with that," I say aggravated as I walk away. OK, Rock's better than I thought but not the greatest if he's willing to leave Brooke in a bind, especially when he grew up with her.

This is not good. I don't want her staying at another hotel, and I don't want to leave in case King shows up and there's a problem. I go back to my room to talk to her.

"Brooke, I can't stay in his room. He has one bed and is planning on finding a woman to sleep in it."

She laughs. "That's definitely Rock's behavior, and I can't blame him after being deployed. He probably needs to get some," she says, giggling.

Damn, she's cute, and she has a crude sense of humor. My kind of woman. "I know this is awkward, but why don't you stay in here with me? You'll have your own bed, and I promise I'll stay in mine.

"I know if I was your boyfriend, I wouldn't want you doing that, but I also wouldn't want you at a hotel alone on an island you know nothing about, and that's where you'll be if you don't stay in here.

"Skyla wouldn't want you staying somewhere else, either, and I need to be here in case King does something stupid. I don't think he will, but it's not in my control."

"I don't want you to think I keep secrets from Rob or that I'm a bad person if I stay in here, but he'll kill me if he knows this. I won't be able to tell him."

"I don't think you're a bad person or girlfriend by sleeping in my room. It's not like you're going to do anything wrong, so I don't see where you need to tell him."

She's a wreck, and I feel terrible about it. Rock and Chase owe me big time. I have to sleep in a room with a gorgeous woman that I can't touch.

"I'm going to go get my stuff before King shows up."

"OK." I run my hands through my hair. Now, I'm a wreck.

Messages from the Past

Chase

It's been an hour since they left. If there's a chance that what's in this envelope could make things better, then I need to see it. I'm torturing Skyla more every minute. I sit up and pull out the papers. The first page is in her handwriting.

Chase,
    These are emails Bud and I shared back and forth. There are many more I can show you. These are some of the last ones we sent each other. Please do this for me. Please read them all.
Love,
    Skyla

Nixie,

How's my girl? When are you moving here, and did you get my gift? I looked high and low to find a mermaid statue with your hair and eye color. OK, really I just looked on the Internet, but it took me hours, and I had to listen to King bitch at me for being on his computer instead of surfing.

He said he can't believe I'm whipped by my cousin. He'll see why I love you so much when you get your ass here, which better be soon, chick. I gotta get back in the water.
Love,
   Bud

I scream as loud as I can. I can hear Bud speaking through this email, and it fucking hurts!

Bud,

I got your gift, and it's the best mermaid yet, so you tell King I owe him for letting you use his computer, but he needs to not be a big baby about it next time. Ha ha! I miss you, too. How many times are we going to have this discussion about me moving???
Love you,
   Nixie

Nixie,

So, when are you moving here, chick? My friends are only going to believe that you exist for so long before they want physical proof. They want to see a picture, but I'll just let them be surprised when you get here. It's worth the wait to see the look on their faces.

Shooter says if you send a picture, then it must include your ass, so naturally I hit him. I keep telling King that if he gets his act together, then I might let him near you.

I've been a bad influence on him, so I need to make it right. You're the kind of girl who could turn him around. I swear when you move here, I'm going to try hard to straighten my ass up.

Love,
  Bud

God, this is gut-wrenching. Why is she doing this to me?

Bud,

It sounds like you have some cool friends who might be a little full of themselves. That means they're probably hot, so I can't wait to meet them, especially this King since he sounds like the one who'll play hard to get.

You know I like a challenge. I hope I live up to the expectations you're setting! You need to quit bragging on me. I'm not that special.

P.S. Straighten your ass up BEFORE I get there. Tell that to King, too. I now worry about the both of you.
Love you,
 Nixie

I chuckle. Skyla definitely does like a challenge. I can't believe she was worrying about me, too. Actually, I do believe it now that I know how compassionate she is.

Nixie,

You are too THAT special. So, when are you moving to this island of paradise that has awesome waves, amazing scenery, and—I can't say hot guys, but definitely hot chicks? It better be soon, so we can surf together.

I miss you, and you know my broke ass doesn't have enough money to fly to Cali. King and I are still misbehaving, but I promise I'll do better if you move here.

King's a great guy. He's been through a lot of shit like you have, and you two have a lot in common. He needs a good girl who isn't just after his dough. He's standing here bitchin' about me being on the computer again, so I have to go.
Love,
   Bud

Bud was right. She is THAT special. He was trying to pimp me out, and I didn't even know it.
I laugh again. He could always bring a smile to my face.

Bud,

Tell King to quit his whining. Do you tell him the stuff I say? If so, he probably isn't going to like me. I miss you ... and King ... and Shooter ... and Brody. Hey, that's the character in Point Break.
Love you,
   Nixie

Nixie,

Yeah, Brody's named after the character in Point Break. You know I have to give everyone a nickname. He doesn't like it, so of course we keep calling him that. I have to torment my friends.

Yes, I tell King what you say, and he knows you're flirting—I mean joking. He says he can already tell that Rock will kick any guy's ass that gets near you. He said you're going to have to be pretty damn hot for him to fight Rock. I told him he's going to want you. Move your ass here, cuz.
Love,
   Bud

She is hot enough to fight for, but more importantly, great enough, and what did I go and do? I left her when Rock said all that shit about me instead of staying and fighting for her.

Bud,

Tell King if he's worthy, then he won't need to fight Rock, and if he's a friend of yours, then he's worthy. But it'll turn me on if he's willing to fight for his woman. You can tell him I said that, too.
Love you,
   Nixie

Nixie,

Now, I know you're flirting. Maybe you two just need to start emailing each other. He said you better be gorgeous, not just hot if he has to fight for you. I assured him you won't disappoint. Of course, you'll be the first woman he pays that much attention to, and it's going to be a sight to see.

So, when are you putting your ass on a plane, chick? The turquoise water is calling you. Can you hear it? When you move here, you need to bring Honey with you.

She's legal now, so I might stand a chance. I'll have to keep her away from Shooter. His charm (bullshit) and Ken doll looks might win her over. He's a great friend though, so I think I could survive it if he did.
Love,
   Bud

Bud, you made sure not to mention the part about it turning her on if I fight for her. That would've been my favorite part to hear.

You were still protective of Nixie whether you wanted us together or not. It still surprises me that you thought I'd be good enough for her. Who's Honey?

Bud,

Please stop making me sound like a goddess. I'm a mermaid, remember? You can make me out to be a hot mermaid. I can live with that.

You sure are optimistic that King's going to like me, so seriously, stop the bragging. Stop it! They're going to be disappointed when they see me.
Love you,
Nixie

Damn, Skyla, I miss you. You are a goddess, and you could never disappoint. I wanted you the first time I saw you on the beach.

Nixie,

Fat chance of that happening. You're my cousin, but I still have eyeballs, so I know you're gorgeous. I'm proud to call you my cousin, Nixie. You have your head on straight, and I don't. I'm never going to find a good woman unless you move here and make me get my act together.

I'm counting down the days! I know King is, too. He won't admit it, but I know he's interested. Shooter thinks he's getting to you first, but he doesn't need you the way King does.

Love,
Bud

Damn Bud, how desperate were you trying to make me sound? I did need that much help. I did need her. I just didn't know it yet.

Bud,

OK, Mr. Matchmaker, you're making me nervous. King sounds mysterious. You know I'm the least mysterious person there is. I might be too bubbly for him. I'm young, too. That's another strike against me. Look how stressed you're getting me! Five months. I'm counting down the days, and you better be ready for me to smoke your ass on the water.

Love you,

Nixie

Nixie,

King says he's smoking your ass on the water, and he hopes it's a fine ass, so I hit him. You two are getting out of hand. I might have to throw some ice on the fire.

Seriously, I got him doing some bad shit after I met him. It's been weighing heavy on me lately. He's out of control.

I don't want to scare you off from him because he's a good person, but we both need to do better. I'm going to put a stop to our bad behavior.

Love,

Bud

Shit, Bud, I remember all these days. I did say that I hoped her ass was fine, but I can't believe you told her, and I can't believe you admitted you got me doing all that bad shit. I could've said no just like you could've stayed out of the fucking ocean that night. We both screwed up.

Daniel,

Yes, I said Daniel because this is a serious matter, young man. You're worrying me. Please get help. Please get help for King, too. He can't scare me off that easily, so I'll be dragging both your asses to rehab if you don't cut that shit out before I get there. Please ... Bud ... get some help. Do it for yourself, not for me.

I love you from the heavenly sky to the bottom of the ocean. Do you remember what I told you about the bottom? It's that murky place where you face your fears and find all that's magnificent.

Yes, I know, it's cheesy but true. I hate to say it, but I think you're in the murky bottom. Please face your fears. I already know the magnificent person behind them, and you deserve to see him, too.
I love you,
   Nixie

I begin to cry. I cry like a damn baby. She cared about me like she did Bud, and she didn't even know me. Nixie tried to help him from across the ocean. She tried to help me, too. It was so true when she said I couldn't scare her off that easily.

If Bud had lived, and she moved here and met me, I know without a doubt she would've been in my house telling me I was going to rehab. She would've cared that much.

Thank God she didn't have to see me like that. I need her. I can't believe I pushed her away again. I told her I wouldn't and I did. Bud wanted us together. He really did.

Dear King,

Bud was right. You're a great person and friend. You turned out to be more wonderful than I could've imagined. You did all the things he wanted you to do. You got your act together, you watched over me and kept me safe.

You even fell in love with me like he hoped you would. I'd wait for Bud's emails, excited to see if he mentioned you ... if you mentioned me. I had a crush on you before I ever met you.

I'd planned to have Rock introduce me to Bud's friends when he came back from deployment, but after falling in love with you and meeting Eric and Andy, I decided I didn't need to meet them. I'd already found guys that great.

Don't you see? All of you are even better than he described. You, Eric and Andy gave me all the things that Bud wanted for me ... all the things I needed.

Then I made the discovery and loved you even more, but I knew it was too soon. I needed you to heal more ... to love me enough not to be able to let me go. Please forgive me for not telling you. Please love me enough not to let me go.

I found the 'King' Bud always wanted for his Nixie. You already embraced the bottom of the ocean and showed me the magnificent you, so please don't hide behind your fears.

The only thing I need you to let go of is the guilt. Let me love you the way Bud knew you deserved to be loved.
Come back to me and love me ... please.
Love,
   Your Nixie

Finding Skyla

Chase

What have I done? I'm an idiot. I have to be with her. I have to go to her and apologize. I get in and out of the shower as fast as I can.

Bud wants me with Nixie, and I can take better care of her than anyone. I'm going to show her that she can trust me. I'm going to show her every day how much I love her. I grab my keys and run to the car.

Skyla

Brooke came to the room earlier to get her stuff. I can't believe she agreed to stay with Eric. I knew she'd like him, but now I'm all alone. It's been a couple of hours since the guys got back here, and I'm going out of my mind.

Wouldn't he have come by now if he wanted me? There's a knock at the door, so I dive off the bed and run to answer it.

"Skyla, I love you. I'm so sorry," Chase says as he grabs me and pulls me into his arms.

He's really here. He came back to me. I wrap my arms around his waist, melting into him. He lets me go and grabs my face, kissing almost every inch of it, his lips landing lastly on mine.

His magical touch brings all the broken pieces of me back together. Letting go of one side of my face, he strokes my hair. He's so gentle and loving with his kiss, and I feel what he's saying.

I feel his apology, the safety he's trying to give back to me, the trust he wants me to believe in. It's all in his touch.

We go to the bed, and without a word, we caress and kiss each other. We do what we do best when we want to show each other our love. I'm encased in his powerful arms, and he smells delicious.

"Angel, I'm sorry I yelled and left you. I can't apologize enough. I should've stayed and fought for you and believed in myself enough to tell Rock that I wasn't the man he thought I was, that I'm better."

"You came back. That's all that matters."

"I didn't think I was good enough for Bud's Nixie. I see now that he wanted us together. Eric and Rock made me see, Bud made me see in those emails, but most importantly, you made me see. You didn't give up on me."

I run my fingers through his lovely hair that I've missed so much.

"You deserve someone who won't give up, and I'm going to prove to you that I'm that man. I love you, Skyla. Thank you for having faith in me, for seeing the good in me before I could see it in myself."

"I invaded your house. If you came back and tried to make me leave, I was going to protest from your bed, and the cops would've had to drag me out," I say, giggling.

"God, I've missed that laugh. I believe you, and I felt crushed when I heard you've been sleeping in my bed, waiting for me.

"I'll be in it every night with you from here on out, and it's not mine, it's ours. I'm going to make the holidays up to you, too."

He captures my lips once again and shows me his love. I'm ready to go back to our home tomorrow, but right now, I'm at peace in King's arms. Right where Bud wanted Nixie to be.

Chase

I get up early and leave a note right next to Skyla as she sleeps. I hate leaving her in bed, but I have to go to my house. I ran out so fast and left all my stuff.

I call the front desk and find out what room Eric's in. Skyla and I didn't do much talking last night, so I have no clue what's going on today.

I knock on the door, and a woman answers in a small pair of shorts and a tank top. I think I woke her up. "Oh, I'm sorry, I must have the wrong room." I turn to walk away.

"Wait, are you King by chance?"

I stop and turn around. "Yes."

"I guess you're looking for Eric. Come in."

I grin. I can't help it. I can't believe he has a girl in his bed. She's ahead of me as I walk in.

"Eric, wake up. King's here."

She's standing next to the bed that's farthest away. He rolls over and looks at me.

"Have you seen Skyla yet?" He sits up.

"Yes. I got here a couple of hours after you left my house. When does our flight leave? Skyla's sleeping, and I have no clue what's going on."

He glances to the clock. "Um, two hours."

"There's no way we can make it. I still have to go to my house. Let me call and move us to another flight. If I can't, then I'll charter a private plane."

Eric holds his arm out. He has no shirt on and is covered waist down with a sheet.

"Brooke, Chase. Chase, Brooke."

I smile at her. "Hi."

"Hi, um, I'm going to take a shower and let you two talk," she says, looking nervous as hell. She grabs a bag of stuff and goes into the bathroom.

I turn to Eric and grin. "You dog. I can't believe you picked up a chick here." I look at the other bed. "You even used both beds, damn."

"You idiot. Shut up! I didn't pick her up. If you had a fucking clue as to what's going on, you'd know that's Skyla's best friend, Brooke."

"Oh, shit. Well, what the hell is she doing sleeping in your room?"

"It's because of a whole chain of events that you started, so she had to stay in here and torture me. You owe me big time."

"I'm sorry, bro, about everything. I didn't mean what I said on the phone that day. I know the last two months had to be hard on you."

"It's cool as long as you stay with Skyla and treat her the way you were before you found out she's Nixie."

"I'm not letting her go. I swear. So, why are you being tortured in this room?"

"Did you not see her?" Eric asks, pointing toward the bathroom.

I can't deny that she's attractive. "Yeah, I saw." I start laughing.

"You're a dick," he says, chuckling. "She has a boyfriend, and he's an asshole. I'm going to have to get Skyla to put some pressure on her to get her away from him."

"You already like her."

"Yeah, I do," he says quietly, running his hands through his hair. "Now get the hell out, so I get a little more time with her before reality hits."

"I'm going to my house. I'll be back, and we'll get home. Thanks, man. You've saved my ass for almost a year. I'll make it up to you."

New Year's Eve

Skyla

"That was the last box," Chase says, kissing my neck. His sweat sticks to me, but I welcome it. He looks mouth-watering with sweat all over his fit body.

"Thank you, sweetie."

"You sure didn't have much," he says with a frown.

"That's all I own."

"You're mine now, so you're going to let me buy you all sorts of things. You're going to have closets of clothes that I get to see you wear, including some new bikinis and lingerie.

"We'll throw some high heels in there and a car, and you'll be set," he says, winking at me.

I hug him. He's cute, and he's mine. "I'll compromise. You can get me everything but the car."

"Awesome. I'll get the car later." Grinning, he swats my butt.

All of us went to my house this morning and packed. I don't have a lot, so with everyone there working, it didn't take long. Chase is determined we're starting the New Year in our house together.

Rock's even here with us. It's surreal seeing him getting along with Bud's friends that he used to hate.

"Are we sitting out back and eating or not? I need to cool down," Eric says, wiping away the sweat on his face with the front of his t-shirt. I glance to Brooke and see that she's staring at his abs.

"Sure, let's go," I say.

***

"Eric's so handsome, sweet, funny and hot. Dang, his body was made to drool over," Brooke says quietly as we lounge in the chairs on the patio.

"I've seen you drooling over it."

Her wide eyes flash to mine. "You have?"

"Yes. You need to leave Rob, move here, and be with Eric."

"I love Rob," she says in a sad tone.

"You don't sound very convincing."

"I do love him, and I can't just leave my life in California."

"You have feelings for Eric, Honey. I can tell. That should say something about your relationship with Rob."

"I'm sure that'll fade away when I get home. I'm going to talk to Rob about treating me better. Eric and I talked for a long time last night, and he made me see I need to ask for that, but he's nice to look at while I'm here."

I roll my eyes under my sunglasses. She likes Eric, but she's under Rob's evil spell, so it'll take a miracle for her to leave him.

We eat pizza, and besides Chase, the rest of us drink beer. He agrees to let the guys read Buds emails. I even have more that I printed. We sit on the patio and pass around the papers. Eric's reading one and looks up at me.

"Skyla, who's Honey?"

I glance to her. I don't think she was aware that she's in them until now.

"That's me!" Brooke yells exuberantly. "He wrote about me?"

I see Eric swallow hard. "Yes, he did."

She jumps from her chair and goes over to him before she reaches out her hand. "Can I read it?"

Eric looks up at her from his chair and reluctantly hands it to her.

When you move here, you need to bring Honey with you. She's legal now, so I might stand a chance. I'll have to keep her away from Shooter. His charm (bullshit) and Ken doll looks might win her over. He's a great friend though, so I think I could survive it if he did.

I see her glance down at Eric. "You're Shooter, right?"

"Yeah, that'd be me. I'm supposedly a straight shooter. You know, I tell it like it is."

"Your charm's not bullshit, and you're way hotter than Ken," she says, giving him an alluring smile.

He beams up at her. "Well, you're sweeter than honey, Brooke."

She blushes, and I see that I'm going to be nursing Eric's wounds when she leaves. We pass around the rest of the emails and tell Bud's dirty secrets, but I imagine due to guy code there are a few left out.

OK, there are probably many left out, but the guys share about Bud's life on the North Shore of Oahu with Brooke and me, and it warms me inside out.

I imagine most people have a Bud in their lives. That hilarious friend or relative who'd save your life but can't seem to put themselves first to save their own. We need to tell that person what they mean to us.

That comical, reckless behavior might be the front for their fears and lack of self-worth that's lurking below. Our words could be the only ones they hear that tell them how magnificent they are.

I'm now lying in Chase's lap. We all spend most of our New Year's Eve laughing, but we also cry, and for once, no one tries to make the tears stop. No one's trying to fix this because it can't be fixed.

This is our healing. We can only take Bud's memory with us and strive to be our best selves in his honor. Chase squeezes me tight and nuzzles his face into my hair. "Baby."

"Yes," I say.

Chase points to my chest. "I only get a small part of Nixie to tuck away in my heart. She belongs to someone else who loved her beyond words.

"I fell in love with a beautiful, strong woman named Skyla. She made me whole. I got my sexy mermaid from the ocean and my angel from the skies. I feel like the King in between. I love you, and you'll always be my Skyla."

End Notes

Thank you for reading *The Mermaid and her King*. *A Voice for my Soul to Sing* will be released late 2013. It will take you on another journey with Bud's friends and family, especially the relationships between Andy, Brooke and Eric.

Other books written by Scarlet Wolfe are *A Week for Love to Bloom (Soul Mates 101 series, Book 1)* and *Brett and Hannah (Soul Mates 101 series, Book 2)*. I'm also looking forward to sharing *Dylan and Taylor (Soul Mates 101 series, Book 3)* due to be released October 2013.

For the latest release information, teasers and discussions, follow me on the web at www.scarletwolfe.com

www.facebook.com/scarletwolfe

www.twitter.com/authorscarlet

www.pinterest/scarletwolfe

Acknowledgements

My husband, Patrick, for helping me see that I'm often my own worst enemy. You're my best friend, honey. Thank you for your love and support.

My family and friends for your continued support. All of you are the rocks I lean on as I find my way along this terrain full of ups and downs.

A big shout out to my cousin, Heidi, for getting me in touch with a cool surfer dude I could chat with about my novel.

A big thanks to the cool surfer dude, Bryan, for all the helpful knowledge.

My beta readers: Belinda, Karen, Kim, Susette, and Todd. You do so much more than give an opinion on my books. You truly build me up with your support.

Eden Crane Design for another fabulous cover. Check her out on Facebook. All of her work is amazing!

I want to give a thank you to my older son, Ryan, who is no longer on this earth. Even after his passing, I feel I'm still learning from him.

He always told me not to worry what other people think. I believe there are those we are close to whose opinions about us matter, but a lot of times, the guilt we feel is from allowing other's opinions to define us.

I was able to begin writing contemporary romance when I was able to let go of worrying if others would approve. Believe in the person you truly are, not the false truths.

Sometimes we just have to give two middle fingers to the world and enjoy this ride called life. We never know how soon it can end.